The War of
the Birds and
the Beasts

The War of the Birds and the Beasts

and other Russian tales

Arthur Ransome

Edited and introduced by Hugh Brogan

Illustrated by Faith Jaques

JONATHAN CAPE
THIRTY BEDFORD SQUARE LONDON

This collection first published 1984
Copyright © 1984 by the Arthur Ransome Estate
Illustrations copyright © 1984 by Faith Jaques

Jonathan Cape Ltd, 30 Bedford Square, London WC1

British Library Cataloguing in Publication Data

The war of the birds and the beasts.
1. Tales — Soviet Union
I. Ransome, Arthur   II. Brogan, Hugh
398.2'1'0947   GR202

ISBN 0-224-02215-6

Typeset by Gloucester Typesetting Services
Printed in Great Britain by
Butler & Tanner Ltd
Frome and London

Contents

Editor's Note

Although the sources for this book are somewhat different from each other, ranging from a late edition of *The Soldier and Death*, published in Arthur Ransome's old age, to the unrevised manuscript of "Omelya and the Pike", it has not been necessary to make more than a handful of small corrections to get them ready for publication. Arthur Ransome wrote as neatly as he fished and sailed; the editor's task has therefore been a light one. I have eliminated, however, a few anti-Semitic details, which reflect social conditions in the old Russian Empire all too exactly, but have no place in an English book for children today.

The texts used are as follows:

The "Chapter of Foxes" contains three items from the 1913 collection of Caucasian tales for which Arthur Ransome could not find a publisher. The original typescript is preserved in the Brotherton Collection, the Brotherton Library, University of Leeds.

"The Costly Ring" is another Caucasian tale. It was published in *Country Life*, 17 January 1914.

"Concerning the Poor Man Covetous", the last of the Caucasian tales, was published in *Country Life* on 7 August 1915.

"Omelya and the Pike" is taken from a holograph in the Brotherton Collection, dated 22 September 1917.

"The Little Cattle" is taken from a holograph in the Brotherton Collection, dated 8 January 1918 (Ransome was then in Petrograd). "The Two Brothers", also a holograph in the Brotherton Collection, was written the next day.

"The War of the Birds and the Beasts", "The Swan Princess", "The Gypsy and Saint George" and "The Blacksmith in Heaven" were all written at Stockholm in the autumn of 1918. "The Blacksmith in Heaven" was published in the *Wheatsheaf*, December 1919; the text of the other tales is in typescript in the Brotherton Collection.

The Soldier and Death was first published, on its own, in book form, in 1920. I have used the text of the third edition, issued in 1963, the last to appear in the author's lifetime. It was published by Edmund Ward, with illustrations by Charles W. Stewart.

I must thank Mrs Ann Farr of the Brotherton Library for sending me Xeroxes of the material in the Collection; Sue Holly for typing it all out; and Arthur Ransome's literary executors, Sir Rupert Hart-Davis and Mr John Bell, for approving the project and commenting on the manuscript. Also the members of Jonathan Cape Ltd who suggested the book in the first place and helped me in all sorts of ways with the compilation.

Wivenhoe, Essex
February 1984   HUGH BROGAN

Introduction

How Arthur Ransome Came to Collect Russian Folk-tales

Arthur Ransome became a writer at the age of eight, or so he said. He was playing a game of ships and the sea with his sisters and brother one day, during which he hit his head very hard on the underside of the dining-table. This accident is supposed to have set free his powers. In the afternoon he wrote his first tale, about a shipwrecked sailor on a desert island.

If this first story foreshadowed Wild Cat Island and Crab Island it was to be many, many years before it was followed by the books for which Ransome is now chiefly remembered: *Swallows and Amazons* and its successors. When he left school at the age of seventeen, and university a few months later, his ambition was to write essays and fairy-tales: essays like those of his favourite, William Hazlitt, tales like those of Hans Christian Andersen. This was in 1901. During the next ten years or so he crawled towards his goal, but it proved much further off than perhaps, in his hopeful youth, he had expected. As a writer he had almost everything to learn, except the lesson of diligence. He was always prepared to work as hard as possible at his art.

As a young man he acquired a repertoire of West Indian stories about the spider-man, Anansi, and used to entertain his friends with these on suitable occasions: after supper at a party, or when there were children about. The stories were always a great success (it is a pity that none was ever written down) and from them Ransome learned the importance of economy of effect and smoothness in narration. It was some time before he could apply the lessons to his writing. He made up fairy stories of his own but they never came to life.

Then in 1912 he came across a collection of translations of Russian folk-tales. The collection was a famous contribution to ethnography — it was not meant for the nursery or the fireside — and Ransome was struck by the fact that although the tales themselves were delightful, the language and the style of their telling in English could hardly be worse. He decided to go to Russia, learn the language, make his own collection of tales and his own translations. He set off in the following year. On his way to Russia through Copenhagen he rededicated himself to the memory of Hans Andersen.

Even then he had a lot to learn. He mastered Russian easily enough, partly from conversation and partly from elementary children's readers, and collected tales from a wide variety of sources: the Russian Empire was a medley of peoples, each with its own lore. He assembled stories from the Ukraine, the Caucasus and Turkistan, as well as from Russia proper. Turning them into good English, however, proved a delicate business. There was so much about the tales that Russian storytellers could take for granted; so much that English readers needed to know, and didn't. Yet, as Ransome eventually explained in his *Autobiography*, 'continual explanation would have been as destructive of the tales as an endless series of asides. The story-teller, if he were to tell the tales as they should be told, had to stand between two worlds and never allow himself to feel he was showing one world to the other. In the end I used to read as many variants of a folk-story as I could find, then lay them all aside while writing the story for myself.'

After many vicissitudes, not least among them the outbreak of the First World War in 1914, he put together the collection known as *Old Peter's Russian Tales*, in which he was able to make many of the necessary explanations by describing the life of Old Peter, the narrator, and his two grandchildren, Vanya and Maroosia. The tales themselves could thus remain clear, swift, uncluttered and magical, for Ransome had at last found his touch as a writer. The *Tales* were a huge success; Ransome's first true best-seller. They have never been out of print since they were published in 1916, and will probably last as long as *Swallows and Amazons*.

Much encouraged, Arthur Ransome set to work to prepare a second collection, but the war got in the way. He was appointed Russian correspondent for the *Daily News* of London, and had to report the progress (or lack of it) of the war in the East. Then came the Russian Revolution of 1917, which was even more time- and energy-consuming. Ransome continued to work at his fairy-tales when he could (they helped to keep him sane under the terrible pressures of the time); in the end events were too much for him, and the successor to *Old Peter* never appeared, though "The Blacksmith in Heaven" was published in a magazine, and *The Soldier and Death* in a book on its own.

Yet the tales which he had prepared were far too good to be left unread in his files for ever. If somewhat grimmer in tone than *Old Peter*, they are no less true to the world of the Russian peasantry, which always had a dark side, and may perhaps serve as a corrective to the almost unruffled sweetness of the earlier collection. Not all of the stories in the archive are published here. Ransome's earliest experiments at translation from the Russian were rejected by the author himself: most of them are too clumsy and wordy. The folk-tales selected for this volume display Ransome only at his best. It is hoped that in this, his centenary year, they will take their rightful place beside *Old Peter* in the list of Arthur Ransome's works.

The War of the Birds and the Beasts

There was a boy called Ivan who lived in a hut in the forest. And outside the hut, close by, a mouse and a sparrow lived in a nest together.

This was in the days before it had been settled who was to live on earth and who in trees. Birds and beasts and men all lived on the ground together. Only the fish kept to themselves, because they were in the water.

The mouse and the sparrow lived in a nest in the ground, very warm and happy, and ate berries and grain side by side. The sparrow brought berries from the trees, and the mouse brought the berries that grow near the ground, and grains of corn, and all the other things that a mouse can get without wings.

All went well until one day when they were having their dinner. It was like this. They had a pile of berries and grain between them, and every time the mouse took a berry, so did the sparrow. And when the sparrow took a grain, the mouse took one also. In this way no one got more than his share. But it so happened that when they had done sharing there was one little shining grain of corn left over.

"That should be mine," said the mouse.

"It should be mine," said the sparrow.

"But," says the mouse, "I fetched it."

"You did, did you," says the sparrow, "but who fetched the berries?"

"Let's share it," says the mouse.

"I'll bite it in half," says the sparrow, "and so we shall not quarrel."

So the sparrow took the grain of corn in his beak. It was very hard and very slippery. He tossed up his head, to get it to one side of his beak, and before he could stop it, it had slipped down his throat.

And there was the mouse watching him and waiting for his share.

"Where is it?" says the mouse.

"I've swallowed it," says the sparrow.

"You have, have you?" says the mouse ruffling his fur.

"It was a mistake," says the sparrow.

"Easy to say that, with a good grain of corn already in your greedy gullet," says the mouse.

And with that the mouse ran at the sparrow and bit him in the leg. And the sparrow hopped on one foot and beat the mouse with his wings. From the noise they made, they might have been a hundred times as big.

And Ivan heard the noise and came out of his hut, and there they were, fighting like anything, and calling each other names.

He was not the only one who heard them.

The rabbit heard them, and ran to help the mouse. The blackbird heard them and flew to help the sparrow. They fought too, and the noise was louder than ever, and was heard by the pigeon and the hare. They took a hand. Then came the dog and the cock, the cat and the owl, the fox and the hawk, the rat and the robin, the bull and the swan. The mouse fought the sparrow. The rat fought the robin. The rabbit fought the blackbird. The hare fought the pigeon. The dog fought the hen. The fox fought the hawk. The cat fought the owl. The bull fought the swan. And other beasts fought other birds. They pranced and flapped and bit and pecked and screamed and barked and squealed and bellowed together.

And Ivan stood behind a tree, where he could see well, and be safe out of the way.

The noise they made brought bigger beasts to the battle. And bigger birds came flying from far away to fight the bigger beasts. The nest of the mouse and the sparrow was trodden under foot by the wild boar as it fought with the solan goose. But neither the mouse nor the sparrow noticed that, for they were fighting, blinded in a little whirlwind of flying feathers and fur.

But suddenly a dreadful stillness fell upon the forest.

The beasts stopped fighting, and bent their heads to the ground, and put their tails between their legs, and waited, trembling. For the earth was shaking with the coming of the Bear, the Tzar of all the beasts. And the birds stopped fighting and stood there, trembling, and ruffling out their feathers, such feathers as they had left, and waited, for the air was shaken with the coming of the Fire-Bird, the Tzar of all the birds.

There was such silence in the forest that Ivan heard a leaf hit the ground as it dropped from a tree.

Then the Bear swung heavily through the undergrowth, and stood there, looking at all the beasts and birds. And the beasts crawled with their bellies on the ground, and got behind the Bear, and waited, panting after the fight, and looking with red frightened eyes to see what would happen to the birds.

Then the Fire-Bird flew through the tall trees, like a great torch flung through the green dusk of the forest. And the birds fluttered away behind the Fire-Bird, and put their heads under their wings, and shivered the feathers on their trembling bodies. And the Fire-Bird, golden and scarlet, with burning breast, and gleaming wings, was alone before the Bear.

Then began the fight.

The Bear raised himself on his hindlegs, and growled terribly, and lifted his black lips so that his white teeth shone red in the firelight that fell upon them from the burning breast of the Fire-Bird. The Fire-Bird spread wide his gleaming wings and rose into the air and came down upon the head of the Bear. The Bear yelled in pain from the scorching of his eyes, and beat off the Bird with slow heavy blows of his great paws. The claws of the Bear were claws of steel, and the ground was red and gold with the feathers of the Bird.

Long they fought.

The hair of the Bear was singed to his skin and as he fought, he groaned in his pain. The Fire-Bird fought silently, beating the Bear with his golden wings, and scorching him with the burning feathers of his breast. And the beasts whimpered as they watched and heard the groaning of their Tzar. And the birds trembled where they stood. And the earth of the forest shook with the trampling of the Bear, and the roots of the trees were loosened in the ground. A wild wind drove through the forest, now this way now that, from the beating of the Fire-Bird's wings, and the tall trees waved before it like fine grass.

At last the Fire-Bird pressed his burning breast on the head of the Bear and blinded him. The Bear in his great pain rolled on the ground taking the Fire-Bird with him. One of the golden wings was broken in that rolling. The Fire-Bird could fight no more. The Bear, blinded and scorched, could fight no more. He stood there, groaning, while the beasts whimpered about him. Then he lumbered heavily away into the forest. The bull shook his great head and went off among the trees, swinging his angry tail. The wolf and the fox and the hare and the rabbit and the rat and the wild boar went their ways. The

wild goose and the swan rose in the air and flew back to the marshlands. The hawk and the owl flew off, the hawk high above the forest, the owl still keeping in the shadow of the great trees. One by one the Beasts and the Birds were gone, and at last none was left but the mouse and the sparrow, and the Fire-Bird with his broken golden wing.

The boy, Ivan, stepped from behind his tree, and came to the Fire-Bird lying there on the ground. The mouse and the sparrow huddled together. Their nest had been trodden under foot by the wild boar, and they had nowhere to live.

"And all for a grain of corn," chirped the sparrow.

"And the Bear, the great Tzar of the Beasts, is blinded and burned," squeaked the mouse.

"And the Fire-Bird, before whose coming the forest itself is silent, has a broken wing," says the sparrow.

"And our home is gone," says the mouse.

"If only I had not lived with you," says the sparrow.

"You shall not live with me again," says the mouse.

And with that the mouse burrowed a hole for himself under Ivan's hut. And the sparrow made a nest for himself in a hole in the wall.

But Ivan cut the bough of a tree, and took ropes of bast, and bound the broken wing of the Fire-Bird to the bough, so that the wing should mend.

Says he: "If you lie quiet for a day or two, you'll be flying as well as ever, and in the meantime we can keep each other company."

The sparrow was taking a beakful of moss to his nest. "Do you hear that?" he says to the mouse, who was sitting at the mouth of his hole cleaning his whiskers. "That boy is not afraid even of the Fire-Bird."

"Why should he be afraid of him?" squeaks the mouse. "The Bear broke his wing."

"Aye, and went off with blind eyes and no hair," says the sparrow.

They would have fought again. But, just as they were going to fight, the mouse looks at the sparrow, and says he: "If we fight, the others will come and fight too, and this time, who knows? they may trample the hut itself to pieces."

"True," says the sparrow, and flew to his nest in the wall, while the mouse ran back to his hole.

The Fire-Bird lay in Ivan's hut. A week he lay there, and covered his breast with his good wing, lest the heat of his burning breast should turn the hut to cinders. His broken wing mended. And on the eighth day the Fire-Bird struts gloriously out of the hut into the sunlight, and the mouse looks from his hole, and the sparrow from his nest, to see the sunlight on the Fire-Bird's gleaming feathers.

"Do you think you can fly now?" says Ivan, and the Fire-Bird did not answer but shook his mighty wings. He looked round at the broken trees and trampled earth where the Beasts had fought with the Birds. And the flames in his eyes twinkled, and says he to Ivan: "Up on my back, Ivan, and we will find something to put on this open ground."

Ivan sat on the back of the Fire-Bird between his golden wings, and the Fire-Bird flew up out of the clearing in the forest, and over the tops of the tall trees. And down below in the forest the beasts grumbled silently to themselves as they heard the flapping of his wings, and blinked when they looked up through the leaves and saw him pass far overhead like a blazing bit out of the sun. The blind Bear growled under his breath and lifted his scorched head, and a ray of heat from the burning breast of the Bird fell on the Bear's head, and the Bear put his head between his paws, and whimpered wretchedly.

But Ivan, sitting up there between the wings of the Fire-Bird, sang aloud as they flew through the blue air, beyond the forest, beyond the plains, beyond the blue hills, and the marshlands and the sea that lie behind the hills.

And the Fire-Bird says to Ivan: "Look down, and tell me what you see."

And Ivan looks, and says: "There is a palace by the seashore."

"It is the palace of my eldest sister," says the Fire-Bird. "We will rest there, and drink tea with my eldest sister."

The Fire-Bird dropped from the sky like a falling star, while Ivan caught his breath.

In the doorway of the palace stood a Princess, as straight as a fir and as slender as a birch tree. She moved like a woman, but she was made of fine gold, and her bare arms shone in the sunlight, like the feathers of the Bird, her brother.

"Welcome, brother," says the Princess of gold, and went before them into the palace, and called for a samovar and two glasses, one for herself and the other for the Fire-Bird.

"And a third glass for Ivan," says the Fire-Bird.

The Princess stiffened like a gold statue.

"I will not drink with him," says she, and stands there scornful, because she was a Princess, and her brother was the Fire-Bird, and Ivan was a poor peasant lad.

The golden feathers of the Fire-Bird rustled with anger, and he went back into the courtyard. "Away," says he, and Ivan climbed up and sat again between his wings.

Then the Fire-Bird rose like a flaming eagle, up, up, into the sky above the palace.

"Watch now," says he to Ivan, when he was high in the sky, hovering like a blazing hawk.

With that he bent his head and thrust his beak deep into his burning breast and plucked a feather and let it go. Ivan watched it falling, scarlet and gold, like a feather of blood and flame. It fell, and almost before it touched the palace roof, the whole palace took fire and burned up in a single monstrous flame. The flame died as swiftly as it rose, and left nothing but a dark place of ashes on the gold shore of the sea.

They flew on. Evening fell. The sun went down and the moon rose. Once more the Fire-Bird asked Ivan what he saw.

And Ivan, leaning forward, looked down between the neck of the Bird and his great golden shoulder, and saw another palace, carven and glittering pale in the moonlight, in the middle of a great plain.

"That is the palace of my second sister," says the Fire-Bird. "We will rest there and drink tea."

Again they flew down, and alighted in the courtyard of the palace. The moonlight fell on its carven roofs, and in its doorway stood a Princess, of silver, with her silver arms clasped behind her head, as she was looking at the moon.

"Welcome, brother," says she, and went before them to call for the samovar.

"Two glasses," says she.

"Three," says the Fire-Bird.

"There is no third here who may drink with you and me," says the Princess in her slow proud voice.

And with that the Fire-Bird turned from her, saying not a word. And Ivan sat between his wings as he flew up again high in the air between the earth and the moon. Once more the Fire-Bird plucked a feather from his breast, and it fell, blazing, through the night, and that palace, like the first, was burned up in a single sudden flame.

They flew on through the night. The moon went down, the stars paled and flickered out, and the dawn spread over the sky. Once more the Fire-Bird told Ivan to look down. Ivan leaned forward over the great golden shoulder of the Bird, and shielded his face from the heat of his burning breast, and saw mountains far below, and lakes, and in the heart of the mountains, a palace. The palace was of bronze with green roofs just touched with the first rays of the sun. And in the doorway of the palace was a little Princess of fine copper, lifting her metal arms to the dawn.

"That is the palace of my little youngest sister," says the Fire-Bird as he flew down out of the sunlight.

"Welcome, brother," says the little Princess, "and who is your guest?"

"This is Ivan who healed my wing when it was broken in fighting with the Bear."

"He is welcome," says the little Princess, and threw her copper arms about Ivan's neck and kissed him on both cheeks. And her kiss was the kiss of a young girl, and her arms were soft about his neck.

The sun rose higher. The samovar was brought out into the courtyard, and they drank tea there in the sunshine, Ivan, the Fire-Bird and the little Princess. All day long they drank tea and feasted together.

At evening the Fire-Bird stretched his golden wings. "Up on my back, Ivan," says he. "And you, little sister, pack him a palace in a wooden box, for we have some open ground to cover, where the trees were trodden under in the fight."

"I will give you my own," says the little Princess, and with that she clapped her hands. The palace grew littler and littler. When it was small enough, she picked it up and put it in a wooden box and gave it to Ivan.

"But where will you live?" says Ivan.

"I shall have to come with you," says the Princess.

So they climbed up on the back of the Fire-Bird, and sat there with their arms about each other's waists, holding the box with the palace on their knees.

As the sun set, the Fire-Bird flapped his great gold wings, and flew up into the dusky sky, and so through the night, like a flying fire. They flew through the moonlight and the dark and next day in the sunlight flew down to the forest and the trampled open ground where the Beasts had fought with the Birds.

There was silence in the forest as the Fire-Bird flew above the trees. There was silence when he flew down to Ivan's hut. The sparrow sat silent in his nest in the wall, and the mouse trembled in his hole under the hut.

Ivan and the Princess opened the box, and took out the palace. One of its towers had been chipped on the journey, but they soon mended that. Then the Princess clapped her hands, and the little palace grew bigger and bigger and bigger until it was as big as it had been when Ivan and the Fire-Bird came flying down to it in the dawn. Then it stopped growing. Ivan and the Princess were just going to walk in, when they looked round for the Fire-Bird.

He was gone. While the palace was growing he had flapped his great golden wings, and flown away over the tops of the tall trees.

Just then, as the Fire-Bird was gone, all the birds in the forest began to sing. The beasts moved again in the undergrowth. The sparrow flew chirping from the wall of the hut and began to build a nest for himself under the roof of the palace. The mouse ran out squeaking, and ran into the palace in front of Ivan and the little Princess, and found a snug hole for himself near the larder.

Ivan and the Princess went into the palace, and drank tea and ate cakes and told stories to each other. They settled down and lived there very happily. The Fire-Bird never came again, nor will he until there is another war between the Birds and the Beasts. And that is not likely, because since that time the Birds and Beasts no longer live together. The birds live in trees and under the roofs of palaces and huts and windmills, while all the four-footed ones live on the ground. The sparrow lives in the roof of Ivan's palace, and the mouse close by the larder. They no longer share their food together. And so there are no more battles between the Birds and the Beasts.

The Swan Princess

Once upon a time there was a Tzar and his son was Prince Ivan who grew tired of palaces and went out into the open country.

On the mountains, in the wide valleys he lived, and on the shores of the blue sea. But most of all he lived in the marshlands where there are many birds. He lived in a gold and silver tent that glittered like frost in sunlight. He slept in gold embroidered blankets and in the daytime went shooting with his bow and arrows and set snares for the grey geese and the wild swans.

One day he caught a young swan, wearing her first white feathers, as white as clouds in summer. And Prince Ivan, looking at her beauty, could not kill her, but took her back at night to his tent and set her in a wicker basket, to take as a gift to his father, the Tzar. "There shall be no blood on those white feathers," he said. "She shall swim in my father's lake, and my little sisters shall feed her with crumbs from golden plates." And he lay down to sleep under his gold embroidered blankets.

In the morning he got up, brushed the sleep from his eyes, and went again to his hunting.

But as soon as he was gone, the white swan came out of the wicker basket, and shook herself, and stood there as a sweet young girl, as pretty as a birch tree, and watched from the doorway of the tent until Prince Ivan was out of sight. Then she busied herself in the tent like a good housewife, and made dishes ready of all kinds, and laid them on the table at evening, a dinner for Prince Ivan when he should come home. And, as she heard him coming, singing across the marshlands, as he came from the sea-shore, she shook herself once more, and turned again into a young white swan, and went back into the wicker basket.

Prince Ivan came into the tent, sniffing with his nostrils because of the good smell of food. He saw the table laid and a dinner smoking on the table. "Who is this?" says he. "Who has been in my tent? One of my little sisters must have been here today. I shall take her the skin of a white fox to make winter boots for her little feet." Then he thought no more about it, for he was very hungry. And he sat down and ate as a man will who has been hunting all day. Then he covered what was left of the food with a napkin, and lay down under his gold embroidered blankets, and slept.

As soon as he slept, the swan turned again into a young girl, cleared the table, was a swan once more, and went back into the wicker basket, where she slept like a lump of snow.

In the morning, when he found the table cleared, Prince Ivan thought he had dreamed his dinner of the day before. He made himself tea, and hot porridge, and went out again to his hunting.

And as soon as he was gone, the young swan came out of the basket, shook herself, turned into a sweet young girl, and watched him until he was out of sight. Then she made him a better dinner than the day before, and, when she heard him coming, shook herself, was a swan once more, and lay in the basket with her head under her wing.

Prince Ivan came in, laden with hares and geese and fat duck. He dropped them in a corner of the tent, and looked round and saw the table, with the steam rising from the dinner.

"Who has done this?" says he. "Come out and show yourself, whoever you are. Who is there here?"

None answered. He listened. There was silence in the tent. He went outside. There was silence in the open country, but for the croaking of the frogs in the marshlands, and the crying of the wild birds.

He sat down and ate up the dinner. Then he covered what was left with a napkin, lay down under his embroidered blankets, and slept. And again the swan made herself a young girl, and cleared the table, turned once more into a swan, and slept in the wicker basket.

On the third day, when Prince Ivan saw the table cleared he knew well that he had left it covered at night. Thinks he to himself, "Today I shall know who plays housewife for me." And he took his bow and arrow and went out as if he were going to his hunting. And as soon as he was gone, the white swan came out of the basket, shook herself, and was a young girl, and watched from the door of the tent until Prince Ivan was out of sight. Then she set about making a dinner for him that should be even better than the other two.

But Ivan the Prince, as soon as he was out of sight, went no further. He waited a little, and then came back quickly and quietly, like a hunter after wild goats, making no noise with his feet, and keeping close in the hollows of the ground, so that even if the swan girl had been looking for him, she would not have seen him. And Ivan the Prince crept up to the door of his tent, and listened, and he could hear the clatter of dishes, and the swan girl, singing a little bird-song as she went about her work.

He waited till he heard that she was near the doorway of the tent, and then leapt through the doorway and caught her in his arms. And she looked at him with frightened eyes, and cried like a lost bird, and struggled in his arms.

She twisted and twisted in his arms, and twisted into a strip of gold cloth. And Ivan the Prince stood there startled with nothing in his hands but a strip of gold cloth. "Where is she?" he cried, and tore the gold cloth in half. "Where is she?" he cried again, with a bit of gold cloth in each hand. "Oh, that she would be here again, as I saw her here just now."

And with that the gold cloth was gone, and there stood the swan maiden, as pretty as a birch tree, and on the floor about his feet were white swan feathers blowing hither and thither in the light wind that blew through the door of the tent.

And so Ivan the Prince never went back to his father the Tzar. He married the swan maiden, and cut trees with his axe, while she gathered moss, and they built a house together, there in the open country not far from the marshlands and the shore of the blue sea. And the house had a yard and a hut in the yard, and there came an old woman out of the marshes, and lived in the hut and guarded the house when Prince Ivan and the swan maiden went walking together.

And near the end of the winter a little son was born to them, and Ivan the Prince had never been so happy, as when he came home from his day's hunting, stamping the snow from his boots, and then going in quietly to find his swan maiden singing to her baby, rocking the cradle with her foot while the old hag minded the fire.

But as the winter wore away, the swan maiden no longer sang to her baby. At night she sat and looked into the fire and in the daytime she used to go to the door of the little house, and look far away, above the bare trees and the windy clouds into the blue sky.

At last, one morning, the old hag who lived in the yard caught Ivan the Prince by his sleeve, as he was going out hunting. "Listen," says she. "The spring has come. You must watch your young wife or lose her. Do not go far from the house."

And Prince Ivan looked back to the little house, and there at the door was his swan maiden, looking up and far away into the blue sky, as if she could see the stars in daylight. And on the birch trees near by was the first green of the young leaves.

Ivan waited, wondering.

The old woman left him and went back to the house. The swan maiden stood in the doorway, and it was as if she did not see the old hag as she went in because her eyes were for nothing but the sky.

And Ivan went slowly back to the house and waited close by the doorway. The swan maiden did not see him or hear him,

for she was looking beyond the clouds and had no eyes for anything on earth. She did not hear him for she was listening to the sound of wings so far away that even the hunter Prince Ivan could not hear them.

For a long time Prince Ivan heard and saw nothing as he stood there watching his young wife. But at last he too heard the beating of wings. Then far away he could see them coming, a flock of wild swans. They flew nearer and nearer and over the little house. And as they flew an old wild swan that flew at the head of the flock cried out to the swan maiden:

> "Ti! ho! ho! my little daughter!
> Ti! ho! ho! my own!
> Let me give you wings
> And strong tail feathers.
> Fly with us beyond the sea.
> Fly with us beyond the blue."

And that was her father flying by. And Prince Ivan heard how his young wife at the house door cried back to him:

"Ti! ho! ho! my little father!
Ti! ho! ho! my own!
Do not give me wings,
Nor yet tail feathers.
I'll not fly with you over the sea.
I'll not fly with you over the blue.
For I have a little baby,
And I have my dear."

And the wild swans flew on, over the marshlands and over the blue sea.

And then again Prince Ivan heard the beating of wings. Another flock of wild swans flew down out of the clouds and over the little house. And as they flew a wild swan cried to the swan maiden who stood in the doorway:

"Ti! ho! ho! my little daughter!
Ti! ho! ho! my own!
Let me give you wings
And strong tail feathers.
Fly with us over the sea.
Fly with us beyond the blue."

And that was her mother flying by. And Prince Ivan heard how his young wife at the house door cried back to her:

"Ti! ho! ho! my little mother!
Ti! ho! ho! my own!
Do not give me wings
Nor yet tail feathers.
I'll not fly with you over the sea.
I'll not fly with you over the blue.
For I have a little baby,
And I have my dear."

And the second flock of wild swans flew on, and away, over the blue sea.

Prince Ivan moved nearer, and then a third time he heard the beating of wings. A third flock of wild swans flew over the house. And again a wild swan cried down to the swan maiden who stood in the doorway:

> "Ti! ho! ho! my little sister!
> Ti! ho! ho! my own!
> Let me give you wings
> And strong tail feathers.
> Fly with us across the sea.
> Fly with us beyond the blue."

And that was her brother flying by. And Ivan the Prince heard how his young wife at the house door called back into the sky:

> "Ti! ho! ho! my little brother!
> Ti! ho! ho! my own!
> Do not give me wings,
> Nor yet tail feathers.
> I'll not fly with you over the sea.
> I'll not fly with you over the blue.
> For I have a little baby,
> And I have my dear."

And the third flock of wild swans flew on and away over the marshlands and over the blue sea.

Prince Ivan moved nearer and nearer till he stood close by the swan maiden, there in the doorway of their little house. And his heart was glad, for she had said that she would not leave him. But just then he heard the beating of wings a fourth

time. A fourth flock of wild swans flew over the little house.
And again a wild swan called down to the swan maiden:

> "Ti! ho! ho! my little sweetheart!
> Ti! ho! ho! my love!
> Let me give you wings
> And strong tail feathers.
> Fly with me over the sea.
> Fly with me beyond the blue."

And the swan maiden lifted her arms, and her eyes shone. For
that was the voice of her swan sweetheart. And she called out
to him:

> "Ti! ho! ho! my own dear sweetheart!
> Ti! ho! ho! my love!
> Give me broad wings
> And strong tail feathers.
> I'll fly with you over the sea.
> I'll fly with you over the blue."

And the flock of wild swans flew down towards the house. The
swan maiden was on tiptoe just going to fly up and away with
them when Prince Ivan caught her in his arms.

And the wild swans wailed in the air, and beat the air with
their strong wings, and flew on and away over the blue sea.

But the swan maiden wept in Prince Ivan's arms. She
sobbed and said to him: "If you had not caught me I should
have flown away with my swan sweetheart to the swan kingdom beyond the sea. But now I must stay with you for ever.
Who will give me wings? Who will give me tail feathers? For
my dear swan sweetheart has flown away."

But Prince Ivan kissed away her tears, and they went into
the little house to play with their baby, and they have been
living happily ever since, for the wild swans never came again.

Omelya and the Pike

An old man and an old woman had three sons. Two of them went to trade in the bazaar, and they left Omelya, the youngest son, behind, and said to him: "You obey the old woman here, and we will bring you a red kaftan, red boots and a red hat."

Omelya lay down on the stove. And the old woman said to him: "Omelya, go and get water."

And says he: "But I am so warm here."

"Take care," says the old woman, "for they won't buy you a red kaftan, red boots and a red hat if you don't do as you are told."

So Omelya took the buckets and ran off to get water. He came to the river, threw in the buckets, pulled them out again on the end of their rope, and there in one of them he had caught a little pike. "Omelya," says the pike, "let me go in the river, and I will do you a lot of good."

"And what will you do for me?"

"Whenever you want anything, call upon me, and you shall have it."

He let the pike go, and, says he, "At my request, and at the pike's command, you, bucket, get along home by yourself." And off goes a bucket with never a one to carry it.

And the folk said, "Hi! Look at this, children. What's this that Omelya is up to?" And the buckets came along and set themselves on the bench.

Then the old woman was for sending him off again. "Off with you, Omelya, cut wood, and bring it to keep up the fire."

Omelya lay still on the stove, and says he, "It's warm for me here."

"Take care or they will not buy you a red kaftan, red boots and a red hat."

Says Omelya: "At my request, and at the pike's command, off with you, hatchet, and cut wood, and you, faggots, when you are cut, come along here by yourselves to the hut." The hatchet went off and cut wood, and the wood came by itself to the hut.

They spent the night, and the wood was all used up in the stove. More was wanted from the forest. "Omelya, off with you to the forest."

"But it is warmer here."

"Take care, or they will not buy you a red kaftan, red boots and a red hat."

36

He went out in the road, and got out his sledge, sat down on it instead of pulling it, and says he: "At my request, and at the pike's command, you, sledge, get along to the forest where there is wood." Off they went. The sledge went through the town. Oi, how the folk stared. They came to the forest. Says he: "At my request, and at the pike's command, hatchet, cut wood, wood pile yourself on the sledge, and, sledge, carry the lot." The hatchet cut the wood, and the wood piled itself on the sledge, and, says Omelya, "Hatchet, cut now a green oak club." It was done, he sat himself on the wood with the club, and off he went home again. In the town there were crowds of folk waiting for him. They wanted to take him. They wanted to beat him to a jelly. They wanted to haul him before the judge. What business had Omelya to go riding about in a sledge when they had to pull their own? And who ever heard of a lad like him with a hatchet that cut wood by itself? Omelya slipped along in his sledge, and when the people tried to stop him, he says, "At my request, and at the pike's command, have at them, oak club, and break their arms and legs." Up jumped the oaken club and beat the whole lot of them. Omelya came home and lay on the stove.

But complaints were taken to the King about Omelya. And a policeman was sent by the King. "Come along, Omelya. The King wants you. What have you been up to? What have you done to the good folk of the town?"

Says Omelya, "At my request, and at the pike's command, up with you, oak club, and break his arms and legs. Why do you come bothering me?" And the oak club smashed the policeman all to pieces.

Then comes a Counsellor. He was clever. He brought along candy, and all sorts of good things, yes, and dried raisins.

"Come along, Omelya, and see the King, he'll give you even better."

And Omelya says, "At my request, and at the pike's command, stove, carry me along to the King." Then the posts of the hut cracked, the walls flew apart, and off went the stove with Omelya to the King.

The King was looking out of the window. "What sort of a miracle is this?"

And they tell him, "This is Omelya coming riding to you on a stove." He came.

"What is this, Omelya, that you have been up to! How many good folk in the town have you knocked about?"

"Your High Kingship, I don't want to say I'm sorry to you." He turned round and was riding off again. But there was the King's daughter looking from a window. Says Omelya, "At my request, and at the pike's command, Princess, come riding with me." And the Princess went riding with him on the stove.

And the King was bitter mad with him. And the King caught them, and shut them up tight in a barrel and fastened it with iron bands, and took the barrel out to the sea, and left them in the waves. The Princess cried, "Oh Omelya, what have you done, and what have they done with us?"

Says Omelya: "At my request, and at the pike's command, blow, strong winds, and throw the barrel on to dry land near the King's house." And the barrel went flying up on to dry land and broke to pieces. "At my request, and at the pike's command, build here a crystal palace." And there was the crystal palace. "And now build a bridge of pearls to the King's house, with silver hand-rails." And then there was the bridge with silver rails. He sent a messenger to bid the King visit him.

And the King came and sat at the table. And Omelya asked him: "Do you know whose guest you are, and at whose table you are sitting?"

"I don't," says the King.

"You are sitting at the table with Omelya, your son-in-law, who came riding by on a stove, and this is your daughter, and now is the wedding feast." And so it was and from that time on the King and Omelya were for ever feasting, now in the King's house and now in the crystal palace.

As for the red kaftan, red boots and the red hat, the brothers brought them from the fair just in time for Omelya to wear them at the wedding.

The Costly Ring

Once upon a time — I do not know where and when — a certain man lived and died. That is an ancient custom in this world — man lives for a time, and dies. Well, this man died, and for a legacy he left a ring; not any kind of a ring, but with a precious stone in it. Behold what kind of precious stone there was in that ring: a hundred towns and a hundred villages was the price of it, and if I had thrown my old wife into the bargain it would not have been too much. The dead man left the one ring, but he left three sons to share it — Kiko, Hecho and Vano. And the trouble was not that they had such names; the real difficulty was, how to divide the ring. If you and I had thought for a hundred years we should not have thought of a way, but the old woman, the mother of the lads, thought of it at once. She seized the ring and hid it.

"If you have it," says she, "somebody will steal it."

"Matoushka," the eldest son, Kiko, began to beg her, "give me my patrimony. Who will steal from me? Why, I stole the eggs of the raven out of her nest when she was sitting on them, and she did not stir."

"That is not much to boast of," said the middle brother, Hecho. "You forget that when you were climbing up the tree after the raven's eggs I took your trousers off your legs and you never noticed it."

"But I am as good as either of them," took up the youngest son, Vano. "Why, I cut the soles off their slippers while they were climbing up the tree. Give the ring to me, Matoushka."

"No," said the old woman, "I will not give it to you. Truly says the proverb: 'Do not give a legacy to a stupid son, for it will bring him no good.' And you are actual fools, stealing eggs from the raven, and trousers and slippers from each other. What sort of profit was there in that?"

Now, over and above her three sons, the old woman had a daughter of such beauty that when you looked at her and for a long time afterwards you had to rub your eyes with your fingers as if you had been looking at the sun. And her mother loved and cared for her more than for her own soul; for she was an old woman of intelligence; well she knew that such a beauty might marry a prince and a rich one at that, and then she, as mother of the princess, would have great honour in the house of her son-in-law, especially if she gave as her daughter's dower the ring that was worth a hundred towns and villages.

The old woman cared for her daughter as for her own eyes, and was for ever telling her: "Do not go, O my darling daughter, into the forest on the Black Mountain. In that place, so they say, lives a terrible, hairy Ndemi giant. If he sees you he will carry you off. How could he help carrying off such a beauty? Think, all the young men, for a week's journey on the roads, pay court to you; like pebbles in the stream are your admirers — peasants, merchants, noblemen, princes — and I have not yet chosen out the richest and most gracious as a son-in-law for myself. How would it be for me in the years of my old age, if I were to have as a son-in-law a hairy Ndemi in the forest?"

But her spoilt daughter did not pay much attention to her. She would take herself off and go after flowers or nuts into the forest on the Black Mountain. And once she walked and walked, but did not come home at night; she had fallen into the paws of the hairy Ndemi.

The old woman sobbed; she wept, she scratched her face, she tore out her hair; she beat herself with her fists, both on the breasts and on the head. She called her sons to her and said to them: "Ah! my sons, my brave lads! Go and look for your sister, my daughter, the light of my eyes, get her away from the wicked Ndemi, and bring her back to me, O my little bright sunshine! To the one of you who does this, to him I will give his father's ring, which is worth a hundred towns and a hundred villages."

Instantly the youths made ready, Kiko, Hecho and Vano, and went to look for their sister. But where were they to seek her in the great wide world? They walked far and wide over the mountains, through the forests, through muddy swamps, over the quicksands and they came in the depths of the wilderness to a little hut. And at the threshold of the hut there sat an old woman so filthy and so ugly that the very sight of her would turn you sick.

"A good journey to you, young men," says the old woman. "Whither are you going?"

They told her. Says the old woman to them: "Well, you will not find this Ndemi, though you wander for a hundred years, unless I tell you the way. But if you want me to help you, let one or other of you marry my lovely daughter. Already for twice forty years she has been waiting for a lover; and where is one to look for him in this wilderness?"

The brothers thought and thought. "There is nothing to be done—we must find our sister and earn the ring." They drew lots, and it fell to the eldest brother Kiko to marry the old woman's daughter.

When the old woman led the bride out of the hut poor Kiko nearly fell backwards. The mother was terrible, but the daughter was still more abominable. And the old woman praised her daughter, caressed her, and told her, moreover: "See, my darling, a husband has been found for you. He will give you food and drink, and will love you, and dress you in garments of gold. And I, the old woman, will come with you and eat his bread until I die. You hear that, young man? If I give you my daughter, you must give shelter to me."

There was nothing to be done. They had to find their sister and earn the ring. And so the young man Kiko married the old woman's daughter, and they went on further, now five together. Oh, far they went, and into dark places, and they met many terrible things. They saw the savage Ochokochy folk,

who live in the impassable forests and do not talk like people but howl like wolves, and do not know fire, which is the gift of God. They saw the water-sprite, the Chinka, as small as a two-year-old child, but its hair is silvery to the heels. They heard the Hadjee crying from far away, the lovely woman of the woods with green hair. And they did not go far from that place where the Tzaritsa of all the witches, the terrible Rokapi, is chained with bonds of hair to an iron pillar, a hairy skeleton with eyes that gleam like fire. They all went on and on together, and came at last to a little hut in an unknown place. And before the hut there was sitting an old woman, still older and still more loathsome than Kiko's mother-in-law.

They greeted her. They told her whither and for what purpose they were travelling. But the new old woman said to the first: "That is right, little sister; you have brought suitors; already my little daughterkin has been waiting for them for twice fifty years. If a loving bridegroom from among these young men takes her in marriage, I will help my son-in-law to send to sleep the Ndemi who has taken their sister and guards her day and night. And if he does not put him to sleep he will never get his sister from him, for this Ndemi crushes a hundred men with his finger as if they were flies."

There was nothing to be done—they had taken it upon them and they had to rescue their sister and earn the ring—so they drew lots, and it fell to the middle brother, Hecho, to marry the old woman's daughter. He spat and spluttered when he saw his bride, old, huckle-backed, and armless too; but he had to marry her. Hecho married, and they all went on together, now seven in number. They went on and on, no small way—farther than from the mouth to the nose—and they saw many wonderful things, and came in the end to a third little hut; and on the threshold of the hut there was an old woman sitting. She was bent altogether into a bow, her nose rested in her bosom, and she was as bald as a knee.

Kiko and Hecho and their mothers-in-law exchanged greetings with her, and told her whither and for what purpose they were travelling. But she said: "Well, I thank you, dear aunts, for bringing me a lover; I have already been waiting for him twice sixty years. What a pity that dear mother is dead; she would have rejoiced on my account. Well, young man," she said to the youngest brother, Vano; "since you wish to rescue your sister and earn the ring, cherish me, a maid, as your wife. If not, you will not see your sister, even though my little younger aunt should show you where the Ndemi lives, even though my other aunt still has the herb her grandmother left her which has the power of putting that Ndemi to sleep. How will you bring the herb near him if I do not help you? Offer it to him? Why, he tears every stranger instantly asunder. But me he will not touch, because I am his gossip, and from old times have kept my friendship with him. I will put him to sleep with the herb, and bring you your sister. Only marry me, sweetheart, if you please!"

What was to be done? When the young man Vano only thought of such a wife he turned sick at once. But there was no escape from the marriage. They had to rescue their sister and earn the ring. And his elder brother said to him: "What! Are we to have married our old hags for nothing? Marry, you also. It will be all the easier for you. At least you will have no mother-in-law."

The young man Vano married the old woman who for twice sixty years had been waiting for a lover. She said to him and his brothers: "Now wait for me here; in three days' time

I will come back and bring you your sister alive and in good health."

And she went off. As she said, so she did. In exactly three days she came back and brought the young men their sister, alive and in good health. The brothers were about to rejoice over their sister—kissing and embracing each other—but the old women put a sudden stop to all that.

"There is no time for that sort of thing," they said, "we must escape. We have a long way before us, and the Ndemi has only fallen asleep for seven days and for seven nights. He will wake up, he will overtake us, no one of us will escape from death, unless we reach a place where many people dwell."

And they all started off, now nine in number, on the return journey. The seven days passed, during which the Ndemi

slept, but they had not nearly reached the places where men live. And suddenly thunder sounded in the mountains behind them, the tall trees shook from side to side and cracked, and rocks rolled from the tops of the hills.

"Oh misfortune!" cried the old women, "that Ndemi has waked and is pursuing us."

And the mother-in-law of the eldest brother, Kiko, flung a spindle behind her. There rose up tall, tall mountains, to the very sky, and the Ndemi had to pass over them. The travellers ran on. Suddenly the wind howled again behind them, the earth shook; the Ndemi had passed over the mountains, and was overtaking them. The mother-in-law of the middle brother, Hecho, flung behind her a comb. There grew up behind them, for a three-day journey, thick black forests; a snake could not crawl between the trees. But through that

forest the terrible Ndemi forced his way, and broke a road for himself—it is still to be seen—and once more overtook the travellers. Then the wife of the youngest brother, Vano, flung a looking-glass behind her, and there spread behind them a wide sea. The forest-living Ndemi could not go into the water, and so he stopped on the shore. And then quickly they came in sight of the dwelling places of men, and after that the brothers, with their sister, with their wives, and with their mothers-in-law, made their way to their own village.

The old mother rejoiced unspeakably over her beloved daughter, and without dispute gave her sons their father's ring, that was worth a hundred towns and a hundred villages. And then there began among the brothers a quarrel as to which of them was the owner of the ring. The eldest brother, Kiko, said: "If I had not married, how should we have learnt where to find our sister? Yes, and my mother-in-law was the first to think how to stop the Ndemi when he was overtaking us. Mine is the ring!"

"What of that!" said the middle brother Hecho. "If I had not married and my mother-in-law had not given the herb of sleep, how should we have taken our sister from the Ndemi? I will not give up the ring."

Nor would the youngest brother, Vano, give way. "I," says he, "am the youngest, but my wife is older than either of yours, and on that account I should receive our father's ring. Besides, my wife brought our sister to us, and she put the Ndemi to sleep, and she, too, it was who finally put an end to his pursuit of us."

So the quarrel went on—oh misfortune! They went from words to deeds; they came to blows; wives took their husbands' parts, mothers their daughters'. Clamour, uproar, yelping; the women, as is the custom, tugged at each other's hair. Well, they fought and fought, and saw at last that however much they struggled there would be no end to their dispute. So they took the ring and went into the village, in order that the old men should come together and decide between them.

The old men came together, drank wine, which the brothers provided for them, and began to judge the matter. From the redness of the sky in the morning to the redness of the sky at night, they all sat there, forming their opinions, disputing and being reconciled. In the end they adjudged that the ring should be divided equally among the three brothers. They looked for the ring. It was nowhere to be found. Someone had stolen it. Some said that a thief had come to the village and in the bustle had stolen the ring; others that they had seen how the raven from whose nest Kiko had stolen the eggs had flown away with the ring. But who knows the truth? The ring was lost that was worth a hundred towns and a hundred villages; it was lost and has not yet been found.

And the young brothers, Kiko, Hecho and Vano, were left without riches and with ancient wives. The two elder had mothers-in-law as well. I should like to tell you that their old wives turned into young and beautiful princesses, but what is the use of telling you if it did not happen. You may say "Honey, Honey" for all you are worth, and there will be no sweetness in your mouth.

And as for their sister, rich people no longer wanted to marry her. There is no more honour for a maiden if she has been taken from her father's house, even if by a Ndemi of the forest. Indeed I, a poor man, married her from pity and not at all gladly. My old woman has such a character. Ah me!

Anyone can see that she brought all the wickedness of the Ndemi away with her. And so I am ready to give her for nothing, with the tale into the bargain. Anybody want her, good people? Be so kind. But if you will not please an old man in this way, at least do not send him away without a present on account of the story.

A Chapter of Foxes

The Fox and the Jackal

Once upon a time the little hungry Jackal was trotting in the fields, when he met the Fox who was going along carrying a little bit of paper in his teeth.

"Good evening, my dear," says the Fox, "whither are you hurrying?"

"I do not myself know whither. Wherever there is food to be had."

"Now if you yourself do not know, we will go together. There close at hand a flock of lambs is grazing. We will carry one off for our dinner."

"There is nothing better than lamb," says he, "only there are very vicious dogs about."

"But what of this that I have in my teeth? Do you know what this paper is?"

"How can I tell? I am no scholar."

"Look you. It is an order that the dogs are not to bite anybody if he wishes to eat the lambs. Go ahead, my good friend, and pick the best."

The Jackal rushed into the middle of the flock. As soon as the dogs saw him they leapt upon him and began to tear him to pieces. They worried him so that the fur flew! And he yelled out:

"Ai! Ai! O Fox! Give quickly thy order, quickly I beg thee ... Oh my pain ... "

"Ah," said the Fox, "do not complain. Who knows these dogs?" he shouted to the Jackal. "They do not wish, I see, to read or to listen. You must get out of it, my friend, by yourself, and as well as you can."

And he ran away.

The Fox and the Barkantz

A Barkantz is a little lean hairy devil who walks with his feet turned backwards. There was in hell a Barkantz-Dev so cunning that every day he carried in baskets to Satan the people he had deceived. And this Barkantz grew proud: "There is nothing," he thought, "in the world, which I have not deceived." Among devils thought is speech: all one. And, behold, a little devil heard his thought, and said:

"I have heard that of all things in the world the Fox is the most cunning. Have you tried to compete with him?"

The crafty Barkantz immediately sprang out on earth, and sought the Fox, and said to him:

"Now, let us make a wager together: he wins who deceives and dupes the other."

But the Fox rebuked him:

"What, what, Barkantz-Dev. It is now Lent. We cannot busy ourselves with such things. Come next Sunday, in the morning during the time when flesh is permitted; then we will contend."

On the following Sunday the Barkantz hurried up to the Fox. He was standing by his hole, leaning his back against an enormous rock. He saw the Barkantz and cried out:

"Clear off, and do not get in the way. Never shall I be able

to contend with you in cunning. You see I am holding up this rock so that it shall not crush in my earth. I cannot abandon it even for your sake: and, moreover, I have no sack for my trick; I have left it at home."

"Allow me; I will hold up the rock," says the Barkantz-Dev, "while you run for the sack."

The Fox agreed. The Barkantz-Dev supported the rock with his shoulder, and thought: "At this point I will loose the rock and let it crush the Fox."

He loosed it. The rock stood, as it stood before.

"Well now, get along with you, stupid Barkantz," cried the Fox from his earth, "you are fooled already."

"Ah, Satan commend me not," said the Barkantz, "truly you have tricked me this time. Let us try once more, and not count the matter as settled."

"What next?" replied the Fox. "Would you like me to take you to the river and bring you back again and not allow you to drink?"

The Barkantz-Dev set off with the Fox on this wager. They went to the river. They came to it. Suddenly the Fox looked round and said:

"But where are the witnesses?"

"What witnesses?" asked the Barkantz-Dev.

"Why you will say that you drank the water: I shall say that you did not drink. And so there will be no issue to our wager. We will go and seek witnesses."

They went back again. They passed by the Fox's earth and the Fox said:

"O Barkantz, were you just now beside the river?"

"I was."

"And did you drink the water?"

"No."

"Well, what more do you want? Get away home, and in future do not have the impertinence to contend with me."

The Black Fox

In a certain village near that place where the river Tiberda flows into the Kuban, where, they say, there are stones from the old castle of Chuan and Sinta, there lived in the old days an elderly man, by name Sheraluko, and he had a son, Shamil.

Now this Shamil was the most courageous of men, a tireless walker, a faultless marksman, but he had no luck. And without luck, do what you may, you will not succeed, and however well you aim you will only waste your bullets on the crows.

So it was with Shamil: he grew to manhood but acquired nothing for himself save a tattered kaftan.

It happened that Shamil went out for a whole week and killed nothing: no wild beast, no bird came in his way, and he turned home with an empty bag, scarcely alive from starvation. He turned home, but the old man, Sheraluko, his father, was already dead from hunger.

The young man wept from grief and from bitterness at his fate.

"Oh God!" said he. "Where then is thy truth? The idle ones, women in men's caps, give life and rejoice and feed their parents, but as for me, do what I will, my hair has gone grey from age, and the only end has been that I have killed my old father from hunger."

And Shamil left those parts, going whither his eyes led him. He went over our mountain, over the mountain of the crows, over the mountain of the magpies. He travelled as much country as there is between the mouth and the nose. He looked round; above him on a rock an eagle was sitting.

"Very well," thought Shamil. "If an eagle, then an eagle." And he took aim. But the eagle spoke to him in the voice of a man:

"Stay, O hunter Shamil, and do not kill me! What sort of food is my flesh? Better that I should drive up a goat for you and be able to be of use to you again."

Shamil lowered his gun and the dark-blue eagle rose and flew away and drove up to him a wild goat. When the huntsman shot it and began to prepare its flesh, the Eagle flew down to him, perched on a stone beside him and said:

"Shamil, here is a feather for you from my wing. If you think that I can be of service to you, burn this feather, and I will immediately fly to you, though you should be at the ends of the world."

The hunter took and hid away the feather, and went on. He had not gone far when suddenly a wild he-goat leapt out directly in front of him, and stood as if rooted to the ground at seeing a man.

Shamil was just throwing up his gun, when the he-goat spoke to him in the voice of a man:

"Do not shoot me, O Shamil; you are satisfied and you have still food to spare. Take rather a tuft of hair from my beard; if I can be of service to you, singe it, and I will appear, even if you should be beyond the seven seas."

Shamil spared the life of the he-goat, took a tuft of hair from him, and went on further.

He went on and on. He went far, he went a long way, God alone knows how far, he exhausted himself with weariness and hunger, and came at last to the great river Edil, or Volga, which, beyond the wandering Calmucks, flows into the Caspian Sea. Shamil lay down on the bank and looked into the water. He looked, and close under the bank a great Pike was quietly resting. He thrust his hand into the water of the river, caught the Pike by the gills, jerked it out on the bank, and was just going to drive a dagger into it, when the Pike spoke in the voice of a man:

"Do not stab me, O hunter Shamil! Poor sort of food is my pike's flesh. Better for me to drive up to you as many little fish as you can want, and be able to be of use to you again."

Shamil granted this, and spared it. The Pike dived into the river, splashed with its tail, and Shamil had not time to look round before little fish came to the bank in crowds. So closely they came that you could see nothing in the water but the

backs of fish. And from the midst of them the Pike spoke to him:

"O Shamil, step upon the backs of the fish and do not be afraid. On them, as if on dry land, you shall go over to the other bank."

And Shamil crossed over the great river Edil on the fish as if on a bridge. The Pike gave him one of its little scales and said:

"Take this scale. If I can be of service to you, burn it in the fire, and I will appear, though you should be on the summit of Oshchamach where as yet no human foot has trod."

The hunter went on further, over desert plains and deep sands. He had not eaten or drunk for a whole day when suddenly from a mound leapt out a black Fox. Shamil took aim with his gun, but it called out to him:

"Hold! Do not shoot me, O Shamil the hunter! My flesh is not good and I can be of service to you."

The marksman lowered his gun, and the Fox said:

"Keep always straight on along the track on which you are going. You will come to a great town where the Princess has already been the death of ninety and nine suitors. Fearlessly ask her in marriage. When, unavoidably, the last difficulty is upon you, then burn in the fire this hair from my tail—it is the only white one of all that I have—and I will appear to help you, even though you should be above the seventh cloud."

He spoke and disappeared, as if he had sunk into the earth. Shamil hid away the white hair from the black Fox and went on further without eating. For twelve whole days he neither ate nor drank but always went on and on. And the further he went the braver and the gayer he grew. He came to a big town, white and red. He almost danced.

"May you live long yet, baboushka," said Shamil to an old woman whom he met. "May you yet be the delight of two husbands!"

"What are husbands to me, my son! I have already out-lived five. Whither are your legs carrying you?"

Shamil told her, and the old woman said:

"In our town lives that very Princess who has already been the ruin of ninety-nine suitors. She orders each of her suitors to hide himself three times. If she finds him all three times he loses his head from his shoulders. If even once she fails to find him, that man will she take as her husband. Only how should she fail to find him when she has, so they say, a magic tube, through which she sees every grain of dust in all the world? The Princess is of unspeakable loveliness."

"Well, I shall go and ask her in marriage, for it is all the same to me," said Shamil.

"Ah, handsome one, do not go, unless you have a spare head in your pocket. But if you go, do not forget; you are the hundredth suitor; the Princess will allow the hundredth to hide a fourth time. Then remember me."

The old woman was and she was not. She vanished, only at a corner it was as if there flashed the tail of a black Fox.

Shamil went up to the Tzar's palace, and told the Tzar that he wished to be a suitor for his daughter. The Tzar was a kind man. For a long time already he had been tired of seeing them cut off the heads of young suitors on account of the Princess. Moreover Shamil was pleasing to him, and he began to dissuade him.

"No," said Shamil. "My life is such that should your daughter cut off my head, it will be no loss to me."

And the Princess called from another room:

"Round my garden runs a hedge which is not yet quite finished. On ninety-nine stakes are the heads of my suitors, but the hundredth stands uncrowned. Your head will fit this stake precisely. Well, rest today from the road, and tomorrow hide for the first time."

All night long Shamil considered where best to hide, and could think of nowhere. In the morning he walked out in the country and remembered the eagle's feather. He kindled a fire, burned the feather: the eagle came flying.

"What do you need, O hunter Shamil?"

"Hide me, if you can, so that the Princess shall not find me."

"Get on my back."

And the Eagle took him to the far-away mountain Gurdjeesh, where its nest was, hid him in its nest, and sat itself above him.

In the morning the Princess went out on the roof and began to look round with her magic tube. She looked to the right, she looked to the left, before and behind, above and below: she did not see Shamil. Midday came and she saw him: how the Eagle hid the hunter in its nest but had not noticed that a corner of his kaftan could just be seen. By this little corner the Princess found Shamil.

The next morning Shamil burnt the goat's hairs. The goat was instantly before him.

"Oh hide me," said Shamil, "so that the Princess shall not perceive me."

The Goat took him into the far-away hills, and hid him in a narrow cave, and itself blocked up the entrance. All day long the Princess sought for the hunter and could not see him. It was already near evening when the Goat shook a fly from its head: and the Princess found Shamil.

On the third day he summoned the Pike. The Pike swallowed him and went off with him into the river Edil, into a deep pool. The Princess looked and looked, from early morning till the evening. The sun was actually setting and Shamil was nowhere to be seen. She was just going to put away the tube, when she looked round. The Pike held out no longer, opened its jaws to swallow a fish, and there was Shamil sitting in the Pike.

"So that is where he got to," said the Princess. "Well, he is clever, but all the same tomorrow he will be without a head."

Shamil presented himself before the Princess and asked her to allow him to hide another time, the fourth. Perhaps because he was pleasing to her, or because he was the hundredth, or because the Tzar, her father, asked her, she agreed.

"Very well," she said, "hide yourself for the last time. It is

all the same. If not tomorrow then on the day after tomorrow, you will be without a head."

And Shamil, the hunter, this time became thoughtful. It was not terrible to him to die, but it was terrible not to win the Princess. He went in the morning into the country, and set fire to his last hope, the fox's hair. Scarcely was the hair alight before the fox was beside him.

"Good day," said he. "And what do you wish?"

"Now, O Fox, save me," begged Shamil. "The unavoidable difficulty has come upon me. I must hide from the Princess or she will not take me for her husband."

The black Fox unfastened the sack of his wiles and turned into a red-bearded Jew, and made Shamil a flea. As soon as the Princess was awake the Jew went up close to the palace and cried out:

"Behold! Fine wares for the young Princess! See my fine wares!"

The Princess heard and ordered that the merchant should be summoned. He undid his bundle of goods, and Shamil the flea hopped out, and hid in the bosom of the Princess, under her bodice, and sat there, dissembling himself.

All day the Princess looked from the roof of the palace. The evening came, the sun set, black night began, and no Shamil anywhere to be found. The Princess clutched her magic tube, and in vexation dashed it on the stones. The Tzar, her father, came and asked her:

"Well, little daughter, have you found the young man?"

"No, batiushka, he has outwitted me. Most probably he is frightened and will not even now show his face."

Instantly the Flea leapt from under the Princess's bodice, fell on the ground—and Shamil stood before the Princess.

"No, Princess, here I am! All day long as a little flea I have hidden in your white bosom."

The Princess grew red. But the Tzar, her father, rejoiced, and laughed till his sides shook.

"You are outwitted," said he, "little daughter. You have had enough of sitting unwed. Marry the cunning one. He will make a good husband for you."

And the poor hunter Shamil married the Princess. And he became Tzar on the death of his father-in-law. Cleverly he ruled his state, and vanquished all his enemies.

Concerning the Poor Man Covetous

The poor man, Avner, and his wife, Iska, had seven children, and nothing with which to feed them. Things came in the end to such a point that their little youngest son grew weaker, and yet weaker, until he was at the point of death from hunger.

"Well get out of the house," said Iska to her husband; "perhaps you do not know that, according to the custom, it is not permissible for a father to be present at the death of his child? Go along, solicit alms, or we shall all die of hunger."

Avner set out. He wandered this way and that; nobody gave him a morsel of bread, for his people were as poor as himself. He was just going to turn back to his hut, when suddenly there came to meet him a venerable old man, well dressed in the ancient manner, with stern eyes. This old man called the beggar, and questioned him: was he of the true faith, did he obey all the rules of the Sabbath, did he not eat forbidden food? All these things he inquired in detail. But when Avner confessed that from bitter need it happened to him to sin against the law, the old man took out of his bosom a little copper bowl, and from his pocket a gold three-rouble piece, gave them to the beggar, and said: "This ducat will suffice you to bury your son and to get food for your family until the Sabbath. And on the night of Friday you must place this bowl under your pillow. In the morning you will find a gold piece in it, and so it will be every week, in order that you shall not sin from poverty."

A ducat is a rich alms, and Avner rejoiced in it even more

than in the bowl. Thinks he: "It must be that the old man is laughing at me. What miracles are there in our sinful days?" But on Friday evening, all the same, he put the bowl under his pillow. His wife urged him to it.

"Why not put it there? Put it. It is not as though there could be any harm in doing that."

In the morning they looked, and in very truth there was a new ducat in the bowl. The law, of course, did not allow them to take it on the Sabbath; but it was permissible to look at it. They set out, Avner and Iska, to examine the bowl, a very simple, polished, little copper bowl. Only, on the edge of it was engraved a certain strange mark, and at the bottom of the bowl was a ducat, new and shining. On the next Sabbath there was again a ducat in the cup, and a week later again another.

65

"This is good," said the husband. "It is sufficient for our necessities, and other things I can earn."

"Much you will earn!" replied his wife. "Think! If in place of a single ducat two were produced, why then it would be possible to put something by, and set up some sort of business. Do you know what I wonder? Whether all its power is not in the sign which is on the bowl. One sign, one ducat. Take the bowl to the engraver Nachshon and tell him to engrave another sign on it exactly like the first."

"But what if the bowl is altogether spoilt?"

"What! Because of such a tiny little sign! Tell Nachshon to grave carefully, and not too deep."

The husband also had a mind to see if he could not receive more money. He went to Nachshon, the engraver, and Nachshon the engraver graved a sign for him on the edge of the bowl in every particular like the first. Friday came, and they put the bowl under the pillow. All night long they did not sleep. They could hardly wait till the morning. And when they looked in the bowl they saw not one, but two gold pieces!

"Well! Didn't I tell you? Take the bowl back to the engraver, and let him place signs all over it, both inside and outside."

"But what if it is spoilt altogether?" said the husband. "We had better try once more. Let him again place but one third little sign."

The engraver placed a third sign, and on the next Sabbath there appeared three ducats. After that the husband was no longer afraid. He and his wife began to count together; how many signs there was room for on the bowl, how many ducats they would get every week. They counted a great number. Then they began to think what they would do with the money.

Avner said: "I am going to buy up carpets from the makers and gold and silver things, and cart them to the big town. Good merchants make much profit by that—double."

But Iska disagreed: "So that's your idea! You will ride to town, but I am to sit here and have no peace with the children! I, too, wish to live in the big town. I wish to wear fine clothes, gold, precious stones. I wish to live in a fine house of my own and have many servants. I wish to go to the bath every week and live like the rich merchants' wives."

They argued and argued. They quarrelled, and the husband gave his wife a thrashing. Now, this had never happened before.

Next morning as soon as it was light, Avner took the bowl and ran with it to the engraver. Nachshon, the engraver, looked it over, and considered, and said: "There is a deal of work to this. I shall not take less than three gold pieces."

There was nothing to be done, and Avner agreed to the price. He had the last three ducats still untouched, but there was nothing left of the two from the week before. "We will rub along," he thought, "somehow or other, even if we go on short commons. And it will be for the last time!"

On the Friday morning Avner got his bowl. The whole of it, outside and inside, was covered with signs, and every sign was exactly like the first. Not for nothing did the engraver take his three gold pieces. They began, Avner and Iska, to count the signs. They counted all day, and made out one thousand and fifty and two.

"Oh what a pity the bowl is so small," said Iska, and her husband was also sorry that the bowl was not larger.

The sun went down and the night came, and with it the joyful Sabbath descended on the earth. Iska laid the supper on

the table—nothing but a pot of millet gruel, and for that she had borrowed the millet from a neighbour. It was a poor Sabbath meal. Well, no matter, it was the last of its kind, and the next day there would be the whole pile of gold.

Suddenly somebody knocked on the door. Now, a guest to the Sabbath meal is the ambassador of God. Avner threw open the door and there came in that same old man who had given him the bowl and the ducat.

"May the Holy Sabbath be bright for you, good people!"

"You are too kind, father," Avner replied.

"But why do you make so poor a meal? Why, you have not even lit a candle for the holiday. Does not my bowl help you? Where do you keep it?" The bowl was standing on a shelf close to the table. The old man took it, looked it over, and said: "Truly, insatiable is the heart of man; there is no limit to his greed for gold! Better it is to be the poor man's son, for his poverty is his justification, than to be the son of the rich. Eh! What is that over there in the corner?"

They all looked round at the dark corner, but there was nothing there. They turned again to the old man, and he was nowhere to be seen. He had disappeared, and the bowl had disappeared with him.

And so it came about that the poor man Avner had again to beg for charity. He asked for alms, and said to everyone who gave to him: "Spit in my face, good man, and smite me. I deserve it."

The Little Cattle

There was a lad named Ivan, who kept an inn, on the great road from Novgorod to Moscow. And in those days the vodka was good warming liquor, and the pedlars and drovers and pilgrims going north and other travellers would rest their legs at Ivan's inn, and wet their gullets before getting on along the road. And there was good straw and even soft rushes in the loft where men slept who stayed the night through. And Ivan was a good fellow and was not one of those who are afraid to take a drink themselves so that other men may drink the sweeter. But, for all that, the inn was unlucky. Few who slept there one night had any wish to sleep there again. And fair-minded guests would often go off in the morning without paying, offering blows instead of money, aye, even if fresh rushes had been laid for them, and they given a double share of straw for their bedding.

And the reason for that was the rats and the mice that ran upon that inn like flies in summer on a dried fish, and even built thickets through the straw at night, and filled the quiet of the dark hours with their weddings and feastings and running to and fro.

It was they that gave the inn a bad name. There was hardly a pedlar or a drover who took that road who would not raise his voice to curse his sleepless nights in Ivan's inn. And this though Ivan was a good fellow and his vodka had no water in it.

One night — it was about the time of the cattle fair in

Novgorod—a night with a clear moon it was, and the back end of the year, Ivan was sitting in his inn, waiting for folk to call in and ask for vodka and hot tea, when the door opened, and an old drover fellow came over the threshold. He was just like any other drover, with a fur cap, and a tall stick. He was just like any other drover, all but his eyes.

And those eyes of his were quiet eyes. They did not look at Ivan as if to see what could be made out of him. They looked as if they were afraid of nothing, and wanted nothing.

And the old drover smiled at Ivan, and bid him a good evening. And Ivan smiled at the old drover and gave him the same greeting. He could do nothing else, with those eyes upon him.

And the drover calls for a glass of vodka. "For it's cold travelling this night," says he, "and there's frost under the moon."

And Ivan pours him a glass of vodka.

"You'll have a glass yourself," says the stranger, smiling with those quiet eyes.

And Ivan pours a glass of vodka for himself.

With that they fell to drinking their vodka, and talking of many things. And so the time went by.

And at last the old drover, he fixes Ivan with those quiet eyes of his, and he says, "It so happens that I have not a silver rouble on me, nor yet a copper piece. And so, brother, you'll have to thank me for the vodka. I'll pay you some time, never fear."

Now Ivan was a good fellow, but no fool, and he'd have thrashed the life out of you and me, if we'd had a drink of good vodka, and then let out that we had no money to pay for our warm gullets. But he looked in the eyes of that old drover, and he did not lift a finger.

"God be with you," says he, "pay me when you can. And let us have another glass of vodka together, and think no more of that."

So Ivan and the drover had another glass of vodka apiece, and fell to talking again. And the more they talked the friendlier they grew, until at the last they were like brothers back from the wars, smiling in each other's faces, and it was Ivan who was sorry when the old drover took his stick, and gave him the blessing of God, and said it was time he was getting on his way.

And says he to the drover, as one friend to another, "What are you driving tonight? Is it big cattle or little? Oxen or sheep?"

And the old drover smiled at Ivan, and he says, quietly: "Tonight I am driving very little cattle."

And with that he was out of the door.

The inn seemed cheerless without him, and Ivan got up, and went to the door of the inn, to look after him going down the road.

And there was the drover, striding away in the moonlight with his tall stick. And for a minute Ivan was looking for his cattle, and could not see them. And then, suddenly, he saw the road before the drover was grey and moving. And there on the road were thousands upon thousands of rats and mice, moving in the moonlight. And behind them walked the old drover, never looking back.

From that day on the sleeping at Ivan's inn was as good as any in Russia. There was not a mouse or a rat in the place. The old drover had driven them all before him along the road to Novgorod.

And some time after that, it happens that Ivan had business

with a neighbour who was known for a cunning fellow. And to get the better of the neighbour, Ivan thought it would be just as well to burn a candle to Saint Nicholas and get the Saint's help in the affair. So off he goes to the church, and buys his candle, and lights it, and is praying for help in the business, when, just as he reaches up to set the candle before the holy picture of Saint Nicholas, he looks up and sees the eyes of the holy picture smiling down upon him. And the eyes were the quiet eyes of the old drover who drove the very little cattle on the road from Ivan's inn.

And there, beside the candle, just below the picture, was the price of the two glasses of vodka.

The Gypsy and Saint George

Once upon a time there was a Gypsy who lived honestly and so had nothing to eat. Things went so badly for him that he had nothing to drink, and that was worse. So this Gypsy, he ups and walks along the high road thinking how he shall get a pint of ale.

This Gypsy he comes to a stand in the road, a-twisting of a straw in his mouth, a-listening to the cuckoo, and a-thinking he could well do with a drop of something to make his own throat as easy as the bird's.

And just as the Gypsy was thinking that thought there comes Saint George himself, riding round the corner of the road, on a great white horse, with silver armour on him, and a gold bridle in the horse's mouth, and reins to put the sun out for jealousy, and golden stirrups, and the horse's hooves all covered with pure gold. And Saint George, he was leaning over his horse's neck, and the gold hooves were beating on the road, and the horse was all in a lather, and his nostrils blowing flecks of foam.

And this Gypsy, he stands in the middle of the road, and he shifts a straw from one side of his mouth and puts it in the other with a twist of his tongue, and he says, "Good day," says this Gypsy, "and what is the hurry?"

"I ride to Heaven," says Saint George.

"And what for?" says this Gypsy, stroking the horse's nose and looking at the golden bridle.

"For orders," says Saint George, "how each man is to live, and what he is to do for a living."

"Tell Please-God about me too," says this Gypsy, "and ask him how I am to make ends meet."

"I'll tell him," says Saint George, and with that he clattered off along the road, galloping, galloping, on his way to Heaven, so that there was no seeing the glitter of his armour for the cloud of dust raised by the golden hooves.

And this Gypsy he twisted his straw back to the other side of his mouth, and watched Saint George till he was out of sight, and then he lay down at the side of the road and waited till evening.

At evening by the light of the moon Saint George comes riding home, the great horse going step by step lifting his golden hooves like ton weights and putting them down as though he were tired of them, with the golden reins loose on his neck, and Saint George all of a hunch in the saddle, like a man asleep. And this Gypsy he ups and stops Saint George and rubs his horse's nose.

"You are not in a hurry," says he.

"I am not," says Saint George.

"And why is that?" says this Gypsy.

"I ride from Heaven," says Saint George.

"Did you tell Please-God about me and ask him what I am to do for a living?"

"I did not."

"And why not?" says this Gypsy.

"I forgot," says Saint George, and with that he rode on slowly down the road, with the moonlight on his silver armour. And this Gypsy, he stood in the road, looking after him, a-sucking on his straw.

Next morning this Gypsy was waiting in the road at the same place, a-sucking of his straw, a-listening to the cuckoo, and a-thinking of his thirst. And sure enough Saint George comes riding like the wind on his way to Heaven to take his orders from Please-God. And again this Gypsy asks him: "Tell Please-God about me and ask him what I am to do to keep body and soul together."

"I will," says Saint George, and rides on, and this Gypsy sleeps through the day till late evening when the moon was high and Saint George comes riding slowly back.

"And have you asked him?" says this Gypsy.

"I forgot," says Saint George, and goes riding on his way like a man asleep.

And there was this Gypsy real mad, for his thirst would not bear thinking of, and he had nothing to eat.

The third day Saint George would have ridden by and not spoken to this Gypsy, he was in such a hurry and tear to be on his way to Heaven. But this Gypsy he catches the great horse by his golden rein, and he ups and says to Saint George, "Now, this time, will you tell Please-God about me and ask him what I am to do for a living, or will you not?"

"Let go of my horse," says Saint George, but this Gypsy, he holds tight, and rubs the horse's nose, and asks again:

"Will you tell him?"

"I will," says Saint George, "but you let go of my horse."

"You will forget," says this Gypsy.

"I will not forget," says Saint George.

"Give me one of your golden stirrups," says this Gypsy. "I'll keep it till you come back. Then, perhaps, you will not be forgetting."

And Saint George, he was in such a tear and hurry to be on his way to Heaven, that he off with one of his golden stirrups,

and gave it to this Gypsy. And this Gypsy loosed the horse's rein, and Saint George, he gave a shout, and the great horse plunged, and they were out of sight in a moment.

So Saint George left the Gypsy looking at the golden stirrup, and galloped and galloped, till he came to the Gate of Heaven, where Saint Peter nodded as he rode by, and Saint George, he nodded to Saint Peter. He rode through Heaven and came to Please-God, and took his orders, how this man was to be a baker, and that man a blacksmith, how this man was to be a shepherd and that man a learned doctor with more books than most folk would read in a lifetime and a half. And when he had his orders he was riding slowly through the Holy Gate out of Heaven on his way back to this world, when Saint Peter who was sitting in the gateway keeping count of them that came in, looks up at Saint George as he sat there hunched in the saddle on the great white horse, and says he, "Why, George, you have lost a stirrup."

"Stirrup," says Saint George, "why brother of mine, that's to remind me of that Gypsy fellow away there down the road. I'd all but forgotten him again." And with that he turns his horse and rides back into Heaven, and tells Please-God how a Gypsy stopped him in the road and asked what he was to do for a living.

"This shall be the trade of that Gypsy," says Please-God. "What he gets, that shall he keep, and the way of it shall be cheating and lying."

Saint George rode off, passed the time of day with Saint Peter at the Holy Gate, and at night found this Gypsy waiting in the moonlight at the roadside, a-sucking of his straw.

"Well, Gypsy," says he, "you were right. If you hadn't kept the stirrup, I'd have forgotten you again."

79

"I thought so," says this Gypsy. "But you'll never forget me now. Every time you look at your stirrup you'll remember me. But tell me, what did Please-God say?"

"He said that what you get that you shall keep and the way of it will be lying and cheating."

"Thank you," says this Gypsy. "He said that, did he?" and this Gypsy, he settled his straw in the corner of his mouth, and turned on his heel and walked off.

"Stop a minute," says Saint George, "where are you off to? What about that stirrup?"

"What stirrup?"

"Why, my stirrup, my golden stirrup, the one you took."

"I never took a stirrup from you. I never saw you in my life before," says this Gypsy. "Shame upon you! Here's a great gentleman, and a saint at that, saying a poor gypsy stole his golden stirrup. I've never taken a stirrup from anybody, and how would I take one, tell me that, from such a man as you. So help me God, I know nothing at all about it."

Well, they argued for a long time, and Saint George gave this Gypsy a thrashing, but that did not mend matters. And the end of it was that Saint George rode home without his stirrup, and rode to Heaven next day without it, and has ridden with one stirrup ever since.

But this Gypsy he shook himself, and twisted his straw to the other side of his mouth, and took the golden stirrup out of the bushes where he had hidden it, and went off to look for a buyer. And he sold it, and stole it, and sold it again, and lives well to this day, eating well and drinking well, cheating and lying and never doing a stroke of work.

The Blacksmith in Heaven

There lived in the world a blacksmith who never took any money for his work. He would mend a wheel or shoe a horse for you, and when you would be asking him what was to pay, he would smile at you and say, "Nothing at all, friend," and wish you good luck on your journey.

People came to know that he never took any money for his work. They did not offer it to him. But when he had shoed a horse for them they said, "May God reward you!" and rode away with their money jingling in their pockets.

Time went on, and the blacksmith grew old, and died, and went to the other world. He went walking through the other world till he came to the Gate of Heaven, and through the gate he could see the shining grass of Paradise and the saints walking to and fro upon it picking flowers. And there was the Holy Peter standing at the gate jangling his golden keys.

And Peter looks at the blacksmith, and says he: "Why have you come here?"

"Well," says the blacksmith, "I have died, haven't I? Where should I go?"

And with that the Holy Peter opened the Gate of Heaven, and let the blacksmith through.

So the blacksmith walked through the Gate of Heaven into Paradise and walked there upon that shining grass, looking at the saints and other folk. And far before him, in Paradise, he saw a great and blazing light, and he went towards it and came to it, and saw, as he came nearer, that it was God Himself, sitting on his golden throne.

God saw the blacksmith, standing there with his cap in his hand, and God beckoned to him.

So the blacksmith went up to the very throne of God, and stood at the foot of the golden throne, and waited.

"Many folk have prayed that I should reward you for your good work," said God. "Tell me now how you would wish that I should reward you."

And the blacksmith stood and scratched his head. At last says he: "O Lord God, I need nothing at all. But if You wish to reward me, perhaps, just for one day You would let me sit on Your golden throne, and see the angels walking below me on the shining grass of Paradise."

"Very well," says God to the blacksmith; "sit you here."

And with that God got up from His throne, and came down the steps, and went off to walk and to amuse himself in Paradise. And there was that blacksmith, scratching his head and looking at the empty throne.

For just a moment the blacksmith was afraid; but then thinks he to himself, "I may never have the chance again." And with that he runs up the golden steps, and sits him down on the very throne of God.

No sooner had he sat down there than the world lay open before him. There was no secret for him in the world. Nothing was hidden from him in the earth or on the earth, on the sea or in the sea, and he knew the very hearts of the birds flying in the blue air. It was no pleasure to him, but sorrow more terrible than he could bear. For he saw all that went on in the dealings of men with each other, cheating and lies and hate and little biting malices. He knew each secret thought of everyone

in the world. The whole meanness and wickedness of man was clear to him. He tried to jump up from the throne, but could not. He tried to cry out and curse mankind for the evil of their hearts, but the words were choked in his throat. And suddenly he saw that God Himself was standing there below the throne watching him.

"No," says God to him, "sit you there, and watch and suffer. You, who cannot sit there for one minute, see only what I see. I sit on that throne for ever, age after age, and see all the evil that is done or dreamed, and am patient with it. Let you be patient too."

But the blacksmith fell senseless from the golden throne at the feet of God on the shining grass of Paradise. And God lifted him tenderly in His arms and said:

"Every just soul is patient at the sight of wickedness. But

no man's soul is strong enough to bear the sight of all the evil with which the world is filled. The soul of man is saved alive only because it does not know the whole evil of the world. You did not know what it was you asked of Me. Better if I myself choose how to reward you. This shall be the reward of your good life, that you shall go back to earth and be a good man, as you have been so far."

And God kissed him, and went up the golden steps, and sat once more upon the throne, looking beyond Paradise, and seeing the wickedness of all the world.

The blacksmith, staggering like a drunken man, passed out through the Gate of Heaven. And the Holy Peter, standing at the gate, jangled his keys and wondered.

Somewhere or other the blacksmith lives on earth today, shoeing horses and taking no money but content if people ride on their way leaving nothing behind them but the words, "May God reward you!"

The Soldier and Death

A soldier served God and the Great Tzar for twenty-five years, earned three dry biscuits, and set off to walk his way home. He kissed his companions with whom he had served so long, and boasted of the feasting there would be in the village when he should come marching home with all his .wars behind him. Singing at the top of his voice he was as he set off. But as soon as he was alone on the high road, walking through the forest, he began to think things over. And he thought to himself: "All these years I have served the Tzar and had good clothes to my back and my belly full of victuals. And now I am like to be both hungry and cold. Already I've nothing but three dry biscuits."

Just then he met an old beggar, who stood in the road and crossed himself and asked alms for the love of God.

The soldier had not a copper piece in the world, so he gave the beggar one of his three dry biscuits.

He had not gone very far along the road when he met a second beggar, who leant on a stick and recited holy words and begged alms for the love of God.

The soldier gave him the second of his three dry biscuits.

And then, at a bend in the road, he met a third old beggar, with long white hair and beard and loathsome rags, who stood shaking by the roadside and begged alms for the love of God.

"If I give him my last dry biscuit I shall have nothing left for myself," thought the soldier. He gave the old beggar half of the third dry biscuit. Then the thought came into his head that perhaps this old beggar would meet the other two, and would learn that they had been given whole biscuits while he had been given only a half. "He will be hurt and affronted," thought the soldier, "and his blessing will be of no avail." So he gave the old beggar the other half also of the third of his three dry biscuits. "I shall get along somehow," thought the soldier, and was for making forward on his way. But the old beggar put out his hand and stopped him.

"Brother," says the old beggar, "are you in want of anything?"

"God bless you," says the soldier, looking at the beggar's rags, "I want nothing from you. You're a poor man yourself."

"Never mind my poverty," says the old beggar. "Just tell me what you would like to have, and I am well able to reward you for your kind heart."

"I don't want anything," said the soldier; "but, if you do happen to have such a thing as a pack of cards about you, I'd keep them in memory of you, and they'd be a pleasure to me on the long road."

The old beggar thrust his hand into his bosom among his rags, and pulled out a pack of cards.

"Take these," says he, "and when you play with them you'll always be winner whoever may be playing against you. And here's a sack for you as well. If you meet anything and want to catch it, just open the sack and tell beasts or birds or aught else to get into it and they'll do just that, and you can close the sack and do with them what you will."

"Thank you kindly," says the soldier, throws the sack over his shoulder, puts the pack of cards in his pocket, and trudges off along the high road singing an old song.

He went on and on till he came to a lake, where he drank a

little water to ease his thirst, and smoked a pipe to put off his hunger, resting by the shore of the lake. And there on the lake he saw three wild geese swimming far away. "Now if I could catch them!" thought the soldier, and remembered the sack the old beggar had given him. He opened the sack and shouted at the top of his voice: "Hi! You there, you wild geese, come into my sack!"

And the three wild geese splashed up out of the water, and flew to the bank and crowded into the sack, one after the other.

The soldier tied up the mouth of the sack, flung it over his shoulder and went on his way.

He came to a town, and looked for a tavern, and chose the best he could see, and went in there and asked for the landlord.

"See here," says he, "here are three wild geese. I want one

of them roasted for my dinner. Another I'll give you in exchange for a bottle of vodka. The third you shall have to pay you for your trouble."

The landlord agreed, as well he might, and presently the soldier was seated at a good table near a window, with a whole bottle of the best vodka, and a fine roast goose fresh from the kitchen.

When he made an end of the goose, the soldier laid down his knife and fork, tipped the last drops of the vodka down his throat, and set the bottle upside down upon the table. Then he lit his little pipe, sat back on the bench and took a look out of the window to see what was doing in the town.

And there on the other side of the road was a fine palace, well carved and painted. A year's work had gone to the carving of every doorpost and window-frame. But in all the palace there was not one whole pane of glass.

"Landlord," says the soldier, "tell me what's the meaning of this? Why is a fine palace like that standing empty with broken windows?"

"It's a good enough palace," says the landlord. "The Tzar built the palace for himself, but there's no living in it because of the devils."

"Devils?" says the soldier.

"Devils," says the landlord. "Every night they crowd into the palace, and, what with their shouting and yelling and screaming and playing cards, and all the other devilries that come into their heads, there's no living in the palace for decent folk."

"And does nobody clear them out?" asks the soldier.

"Easier said than done," says the landlord.

Well, with that the soldier wishes good health to the landlord, and sets off to see the Tzar. He comes walking into the Tzar's house and gives him a salute.

"Your Majesty," says he, "will you give me leave to spend one night in your empty palace?"

"God bless you," says the Tzar, "but you don't know what you are asking. Foolhardy folk enough have tried to spend a night in that palace. They went in merry and boasting, but not one of them came walking out alive in the morning."

"What of that?" says the soldier. "Water won't drown a Russian soldier, and fire won't burn him. I have served God and the Tzar for twenty-five years and am not dead. A single night in that palace won't be the end of me."

"But I tell you: a man walks in there alive in the evening, and in the morning the servants have to search the floor for the little bits of his bones."

"None the less," says the soldier, "if your Majesty will give me leave … "

"Get along with you and God be with you," says the Tzar. "Spend the night there if you've set your heart on it."

So the soldier came to the palace and stepped in, singing through the empty rooms. He made himself comfortable in the biggest room of all, laid his sack in a corner and hung his sword on a nail, sat down at the table, took out his bag of tobacco, filled his little pipe, and sat there smoking, ready for what might come.

Twelve o'clock sharp and there was a yelling, a shouting, a blowing of horns, a scraping of fiddles and every other kind of instrument, a noise of dancing, of running, of stamping, and the palace cram full of devils making themselves at home as if the place belonged to them.

"And you, soldier?" cried the devils. "What are you sitting

there so glum for, smoking your pipe? There's smoke enough where we have been. Put your pipe in your pocket and play a round of cards with us."

"Right you are," says the soldier, "if you'll play with my cards."

"Deal them out," shouted the devils, and the soldier put his pipe in his pocket and dealt out the cards, while the devils crowded round the table fighting for room on the benches.

They played a game and the soldier won. They played another and he won again. The devils were cunning enough, God knows, but not all their cunning could win a single game for them. The soldier was raking in the money all the time. Soon enough the devils had not a penny piece between them, and the soldier was for putting up his cards and lighting his pipe. Content he was, and well he might be, with his pockets bulging with money.

"Stop a minute, soldier," said the devils, "we've still got sixty bushels of silver and forty of gold. We'll play for them if you'll give us time to send for them."

"Let's see the silver," says the soldier, and puts the cards in his pocket.

Well, they sent a little devil to fetch the silver. Sixty times he ran out of the room and sixty times he came staggering back with a bushel of silver on his shoulders.

The soldier pulled out his cards, and they played on, but it was all the same. The devils cheated in every kind of way, but could not win a game.

"Go and fetch the gold," says the oldest devil.

"Aye, aye, grandfather," says the little devil, and goes scuttling out of the room. Forty times he ran out, and forty times

he came staggering back with a bushel of gold between his shoulders.

They played on. The soldier won every game and all the gold, asked if they had any more money to lose, put his cards in his pocket and lit his pipe.

The devils looked at all the money they had lost. It seemed a pity to lose all the good silver and gold.

"Tear him to pieces, brothers," they cried, "tear him to pieces, eat him and have done!"

The soldier tapped his little pipe on the table.

"First make sure," says he, "who eats whom." And with that he whips out his sack, and, says he, to the devils, who were all gnashing their teeth and making ready to fall on him, "What do you call this?"

"It's a sack," said the devils.

"Is it?" says the soldier. "Then, by the word of God, get into it!"

And the next minute all those devils were tumbling over each other and getting into the sack, squeezing in one on the top of another until the last one had got inside. Then the soldier tied up the sack with a good double knot, hung it on a nail, and lay down to sleep.

In the morning the Tzar sent his servants.

"Go," says the Tzar, "and see what has happened to the soldier who spent the night in the empty palace. If the unclean spirits have made an end of him, then you must sweep up what is left of his bones."

The servants came, all ready to lament for the brave soldier done to death by the unclean, and there was the soldier walking cheerfully from one room to another, smoking his little pipe.

"Well done, soldier! We never thought to see you alive.

And how did you spend the night? How did you manage against the devils?"

"Devils?" says the soldier. "I wish all men I have played cards against had paid their debts so honestly. Have a look at the silver and gold I won from them. Look at the heaps of money lying on the floor."

The servants looked at the silver and gold and touched it to see if it was real. But there was no doubt about that. I wish I had more in my pocket of the same sort.

"Now, brothers," said the soldier, "off with you as quick as you can, go and fetch two blacksmiths here on the run. And let them bring with them an iron anvil and the two heaviest hammers in the forge."

The servants asked no questions, but hurried to the smithy, and the two blacksmiths came running, with anvil and hammers. Giants they were, the strongest men in all the town.

"Now," says the soldier, "take that sack from the nail and lay it on the anvil and let me see how the blacksmiths of this town can set about their work."

The blacksmiths took the sack from the nail.

"Devil take it, what a weight," they said to each other.

And little voices screamed out of the sack: "We are good folk. We are your own people."

"Are you?" said the blacksmiths; and they laid the sack on the anvil and swung the great hammers, up and down, up and down, as if they were beating out a lump of iron.

The devils fared badly in there, and worse and worse. The hammers came down as if they were going through devils, anvil, earth, and all. It was more than even devils could bear.

"Have mercy!" they screamed. "Have mercy, soldier! Let us out again into the world, and we'll never forget you world without end. And as for this palace ... no devil shall put the nail of the toe of his foot in it. We'll tell them all. Not one shall come within a hundred miles."

The soldier let the blacksmiths give a few more blows, just for luck. Then he stopped them, and untied the mouth of the sack. The moment he opened it, the devils shot out, and fled away to hell without looking right or left in their hurry.

But the soldier was no fool, and he grabbed one old devil by the leg. And the devil hung gibbering, trying to get away. The soldier cut the devil's hairy wrist to the bone, so that the blood flowed, took a pen, dipped it in the blood, and gave it to the devil. But he never let go of his leg.

"Write," says he, "that you will be my faithful servant."

The old devil screamed and wriggled, but the soldier gripped him tight. There was nothing to be done. He wrote and signed

in his own blood a promise to serve the soldier faithfully wherever and whenever there should be need. Then the soldier let him go, and he went hopping and screaming after the others, and had disappeared in a moment.

And so the devils went rushing down to hell, aching in every bone of their hairy bodies. And they called all the other unclean spirits, old and young, big and little, and told what had happened to them. And they set sentinels all round hell, and guards at every gate, and ordered them to watch well, and, whatever they did, not on any account to let in the soldier with the sack.

The soldier went to the Tzar and told him how he had dealt with the devils, and how henceforth no devil would set foot within a hundred miles of the palace.

"If that's so," says the Tzar, "we'll move at once and go and live there, and you shall live with me and be honoured as my own brother." And with that there was a great to do shifting the bedding and tables and benches and all else from the old palace to the new, and the soldier set up house with the Tzar, living with him as his own brother, and wearing fine clothes with gold embroidery, and eating the same food as the Tzar, and as much of it as he liked. Money to spend he had, for he had won from the devils enough to last even a spending man a thousand years. And he had nothing to spend it on. Hens don't eat gold. No more do mice. And there the money lay in a corner till the soldier was tired of looking at it.

So the soldier thought he would marry. And he took a wife, and in a year's time God gave him a son, and he had nothing more to wish for except to see the son grow up and turn into a general.

But it so happened that the little boy fell ill, and what was the matter with him no one knew. He grew worse and worse from day to day, and the Tzar sent for every doctor in the country, but not one of them did him a half-pennyworth of good. The doctors grew richer and the boy grew no better but worse, as is often the way.

The soldier had almost given up hope of saving his son when he remembered the old devil who had signed a promise written in his own blood to serve the soldier faithfully wherever and whenever there should be need. He remembered this, and said to himself: "Where the devil has my old devil hidden himself all this time?"

And he had only just said this when suddenly there was the little old devil standing in front of him, dressed like a peasant in a little shirt and breeches, trembling with fright and asking: "How can I serve your Excellency?"

"See here," says the soldier. "My son is ill. Do you happen to know how to cure him?"

The little old devil took a glass from his pocket and filled it with cold water and set it on the sick child's forehead.

"Come here, your Excellency," says he, "and look into the glass of water."

The soldier came and looked in the glass.

"And what does your Excellency see?" asked the little old devil, who was so much afraid of the soldier that he trembled and could hardly speak.

"I see Death, like a little old woman, standing at my son's feet."

"Be easy," says the little old devil, "for if Death is standing at your son's feet he will be well again. But if Death were standing at his head then nothing could save him."

And with that the little old devil lifted the glass and splashed

the cold water over the sick child, and the next minute there was the little boy crawling about and laughing and crowing as if he had never been sick in his life.

"Give me that glass," says the soldier, "and we'll call it quits."

The little old devil gave him the glass. And the soldier gave back the promise which the devil had signed in his own blood. As soon as the little old devil had that promise in his hand he gave one look at the soldier and fled away as if the blacksmiths had only that minute stopped beating him on the anvil.

And the soldier after that set up as a wise man and put all the doctors out of business, curing the boyars and generals. He would just look in his glass, and if Death stood at a sick man's feet, he threw the water over him and cured him. If Death

97

stood at the sick man's head, he said: "It's all up with you," and the sick man died as sure as fate.

All went well until the Tzar himself fell ill and sent for the soldier to cure him.

The soldier went in, and the Tzar greeted him as his own brother, and prayed him to be quick, as he felt the sickness growing upon him as he lay. The soldier poured cold water in the glass, and set it on the Tzar's forehead, and looked and looked again, and saw Death standing at the Tzar's head.

"O Tzar," says the soldier, "it's all up with you. Death is waiting by your head, and you have but a few minutes left to live."

"What?" cries the Tzar. "You cure my boyars and generals and you will not cure me who am Tzar, and have treated you as my own born brother? If I've only a few minutes to live I've time enough to give orders for you to be beheaded."

The soldier thought, and thought, and he begged Death: "O Death," says he, "give my life to the Tzar and kill me instead. Better to die so than to end by being shamefully beheaded!"

He looked once more in the glass, and saw that the little old woman Death had shifted from the Tzar's head and was now standing at his feet. He picked up the glass and splashed the water over the Tzar, and there was the Tzar as well and healthy as ever he had been.

"You are my own true brother after all," says the Tzar. "Let us go and feast together."

But the soldier shook in all his limbs and could hardly stand, and he knew that his time was come. He prayed Death: "O Death, give me just one hour to say goodbye to my wife and my little son."

"Hurry up!" says Death.

And the soldier hurried to his room in the palace, said goodbye to his wife, told his son to grow up and be a general, lay down on his bed and grew iller every minute.

He looked, and there was Death, a little old woman, standing by his bedside.

"Well, soldier," says Death, "you have only two minutes left to live!"

The soldier groaned and, turning in bed, pulled the sack from under his pillow and opened it.

"Do you know what this is?" says he to Death.

"A sack," says Death.

"Well, if it is a sack, get into it!" says the soldier.

Death was into the sack in a moment, and the soldier leapt from his bed well and strong, tied up the sack with two double knots, flung it over his shoulder and set out for the deep forest of Brian, which is the thickest in all the world. He came to the forest and made his way into the middle of it, hung the sack from the topmost branches of a high poplar tree, left it there and came home singing songs at the top of his voice and full of all kinds of merriment.

From that time on there was no dying in the world. There were births every day, and plenty of them, but nobody died. It was a poor time for doctors. And so it was for many years. Death had come to an end, and it was as if all men would live for ever. And all the time the little old woman, Death, tied up in a sack, unable to get about her business, was hanging from the top of a tall poplar tree away in Brian forest.

And then, one day, the soldier was walking out to take the air, and he met an ancient old crone, so old and so ancient that she was like to fall whichever way the wind blew. She tottered along, blown this way and that, like a blade of withered grass.

"What an old hag," said the soldier to himself. "It was time for her to die a many years ago."

"Yes," says the old crone, with her toothless gums mumbling and grumbling over her words. "Long ago it was time for me to die. When you shut up Death in the sack I had only an hour left to live. I had done with the world, and the world had done with me, and I would have been glad to be at peace. Long ago my place in Heaven was made ready, and it is empty to this day, for I cannot die. You, soldier, have sinned a sin that God will not forgive. I am not the only soul in the world who is tortured as I am. Mine is not the only place that is growing dusty in Heaven. Hundreds and thousands of us who should have died drag on in misery about the world. And but for you we should now be resting in peace."

The soldier began to think. And he thought of all the other old men and women he had kept from the rest that God had made ready for them: "There is no doubt about it," thinks he; "I had better let Death loose again. No matter if I am the first of whom she makes an end. I have sinned many sins, not counting this one. Better go to the other world now and bear my punishment while I am strong, for when I am very old it will come worse to me to be tormented."

So he set off to the forest of Brian, which is the thickest in all the world. He found the poplar tree, and saw the sack hanging from the topmost branches, swinging this way and that as the wind blew.

"Well, Death, are you alive up there?" the soldier shouted against the wind.

And a little voice, hardly to be heard, answered from the sack: "Alive, little father!"

So the soldier climbed up the tree, took down the sack, and carried it home over his shoulder. He said goodbye to his wife and his son, who was now a fine young lad. Then he went into his own room, opened the bag, lay down upon the bed, and begged Death to make an end of him.

And Death, in the form of a little old woman, crept trembling out of the sack, looking this way and that, for she was very much afraid. As soon as she saw the soldier she bolted through the door, and ran away as fast as her little old legs could carry her. "The devils can make an end of you if they like," she shrieked, "but you don't catch me taking a hand in it."

The soldier sat up on the bed and knew that he was alive and well. Troubled he was as to what to do next. Thinks he: "I'd better get straight along to Hell, and let the devils throw

me into the boiling pitch, and stew me until all my sins are stewed out of me."

So he said goodbye to everybody, took his sack in his hands and set off to Hell by the best road he could find.

Well, he walked on and on, over hill and valley and through the deep forest, until he came at last to the kingdom of the unclean. There were the walls of Hell and the gates of Hell, and as he looked he saw that sentinels were standing at every gate.

As soon as he came near a gate the devil doing sentry go calls out:

"Who goes there?"

"A sinful soul come to you to be stewed in the boiling pitch."

"And what is that you've got in your hand?"

"A sack."

And the devil yelled out at the top of his voice and gave the alarm. From all sides the unclean rushed up and began closing every gate and window in Hell with strong bolts and bars.

And the soldier walked round Hell outside the walls, unable to get in.

He cried out to the Prince of Hell:

"Let me into Hell, I beg you. I have come to you to be tormented, because I have sinned before God and before man."

"No," shouted the Prince of Hell, "I won't let you in. Go away. Go away, I tell you. Go away, anywhere you like. There's no place for you here."

The soldier was more troubled than ever.

"Well," says he, "if you won't let me in, you won't. I'll go away if you will give me two hundred sinful souls. I will take them to God, and perhaps, when he sees them, he will forgive me and let me into Heaven."

"I'll throw in another fifty," says the Prince of Hell, "if only you'll get away from here."

And he told the lesser devils to count out two hundred and fifty sinful souls and to let them out quickly at one of the back doors of Hell, while he held the soldier in talk, so that the soldier should not slip in while the sinful souls were going out.

It was done, and the soldier set off for Heaven with two hundred and fifty sinful souls behind him, marching in column of route, as the soldier made them for the sake of order and decency.

Well, they marched on and on, and in the end they came to Heaven, and stopped before the very gates of Paradise.

And the holy apostles, standing in the gateway of Paradise, said: "Who are you?"

"I am the soldier who hung Death in a sack, and I have brought two hundred and fifty sinful souls from Hell in hope that God will pardon my sins and let me into Paradise."

And the apostles went to the Lord, and told him that the soldier had come, and brought with him two hundred and fifty sinful souls.

And God said: "Let in the sinful souls, but do not let in the soldier."

The apostles went back to the gateway, and opened the gates and told the souls they might come in. But when the soldier tried to march in at the head of his company they stopped him, and said: "No, soldier! There's no place for you here."

So the soldier took one of the sinful souls aside and gave that soul his sack, and told him: "As soon as you are through the gates of Paradise, open the sack and shout out, 'Into the sack, soldier!' You will do this because I brought you here from Hell."

And the sinful soul promised to do this for the soldier.

But when that sinful soul went through the gates into Paradise, for very joy it forgot about the soldier, and threw away the sack somewhere in Paradise, where it may be lying to this day.

And the soldier, after waiting a long time, went slowly back to earth. Death would not take him. There was no place for him in Paradise and no place for him in Hell. For all I know he may be living yet.

The Two Brothers

There were once two brothers, Ostap and Ivan. Ostap was the elder by one year, but they loved each other like twins. And when their father died, and left them the little farm and what there was with it, they did not leave each other. They did not draw lots for the property. No: what was Ostap's was Ivan's, and whatever Ivan had Ostap was welcome to make what use he could of it. And so they lived, with never a bitter word between them.

Eh, but it was ill living for peasants in those days. Up before dawn to work for the gentry and slave away till evening, every day alike. A man had no time for the tilling of his own earth, unless he was to kill himself with labour. Only a strong man could live. And so it was that Ostap died, and left Ivan alone.

And Ivan, the younger brother, lamented bitterly. And wept for his brother. For as I told you they loved each other like twins.

He tried living alone, but, when his day's work was done for the gentry, he had no heart for the tilling of his own earth, now that he could not look up from the plough and see his brother at the far end of the furrow.

He sat at the table with his head in his hands and asked himself what he could do with his life, to make it worth living, so that he could face God with a glad heart and not curse his fate from morning to night.

And, thinks he, "I will marry. I shall not be alone all the

time. And even if things are wicked, it is easier for two than for one." And with that he put his cap on his head, and went and asked the Elder of the Village to find him a good wife of an honourable decent family.

A bride was found for him, and all was fixed up for the wedding. His wife-to-be went round the village with her friends, inviting relatives and acquaintances to the wedding feast.

And Ivan thinks to himself, and, says he, "I will go to the graveyard, to my brother, and ask him to the wedding, and in memory of my wedding, lay acorns on his grave."

So Ivan came to the graveyard, to his brother's grave, and took off his hat, and crossed himself, and laid the acorns at the foot of the grave. And he thought of how he loved his brother better than all else in the world, and how he had no other friends. And he threw himself on his face on the grave and said, "Oh, brother of mine, I beg you come to my wedding, for I have wearied of sorrowing alone, and today I shall be married."

He had hardly said these words when the earth opened before him. And there in the earth was a deep vault, and in the vault there was Ostap his brother, sitting and smiling as he used to smile on earth.

And, says Ostap, "Come you to me, Ivan, and let us talk things over."

And Ivan went down into the vault, and the earth closed behind him.

Ostap lit a wax candle, and the two of them sat there, in the vault in the graveyard, talking, as if they had met after a journey, with the wax candle throwing shadows of them on the wet walls.

And Ivan told his brother how hard was life up there in the world.

Ostap listened, slowly nodding his head.

But when Ivan had done, Ostap said to him:

"Truly life is hard in the world. But folk in the world are unhappy because they do not live in the right way. Listen now, how we live here, and you will learn how folk should live in the world above ground."

And Ostap took a heavy, stout old book from a shelf, and set it in the light of the wax candle and began to read, down there in the vault, to his younger brother Ivan who had come to visit him.

And in this book everything was written as it should be. Folk loved one another. There were no rich and no poor, no strong and no weak. All men were equal. And each man called all men his brothers. In that book there was no working for

rich gentry till your back was nigh breaking before evening came and you were free for the tilling of your own scrap of land. Many, many were the good things that Ostap read out of that book. And Ivan listened, and did not think of stirring.

And the wax candle burnt out.

Ostap lit a second candle, and read on. And Ivan listened with his head in his hands and the tears running through his fingers as he heard of the life in this book and thought of the life he knew on earth.

And the second candle burnt out.

Ostap looked up from his reading, and says he, "What about that wedding of yours? Don't you want to be going home? You have been here a long time."

"No, brother, no," says Ivan. "Let me hear a little more of your book. Eh," says he, "but it's fine to think of living like that, among some good kind folk, with justice to be had everywhere and not be carried up by the folk's money bags. Just a little longer, let me think that the world is like that."

So Ostap lit a third candle, and read on, while Ivan listened.

And he heard how there were no wars, and no quarrelling; how if one man had too much, he gave to his neighbour; how there was no weeping; and how men lived like children, trusting each other and God.

And the third candle burnt out.

And Ivan stood up, remembering the wedding that was to be. And he said, "Oh brother, I could listen to your book for hundreds of years and never have enough. But now it will be time for me to go home, or they will be waiting for me."

"Go," says Ostap. And the earth opened before Ivan, and he stepped out of the vault, and the earth closed behind him, and he stood there rubbing his eyes.

He was in the graveyard by his brother's grave. But at the foot of the grave was a huge oak.

"It's a queer thing," says Ivan to himself, "but it seems to me there was no tree there when I came, and yet look at this great tree."

And says he wondering, "I did not think there were so many graves."

He crossed himself again before his brother's grave, and went home, wondering, rubbing his eyes, and staring at all he saw.

He knew the road well enough: but it seemed changed. There were some cottages that he remembered. And the cottages seemed different. There were children in the road and they did not know him. There were old people, and he did not know them.

He came to his own farm. The place was the same, but the building was different. And there were barns and outhouses that he could not call to mind. And people came out of the house, strangers: and he wondered what they had been doing in his house.

And these strangers whom he did not know came out of his own house and asked him what he wanted.

"What do you mean?" says Ivan. "This is my house, and was my father's before me. And my grandparents lived here. I am Ivan. Don't you know who I am? I have been to my brother's grave to bid him come to my wedding today."

And the strangers, coming out of his own house, laughed in his face.

"Eh, good man," say they, "why do you try to make fools of us? Why do you talk empty folly? We don't know you." Others of the village came round, and stared at him and listened. One said: "He has got hold of the old tale, how three hundred years ago a man lived here who was going to marry and who went to his brother's grave and was never seen again."

And the others said, "Aye. We have heard that tale, but we know nothing about you. Off with you and don't come bothering busy folk with your nonsense."

And Ivan turned away from his own house and went through the village.

He knew now what had happened, and that while one candle burned itself out down there in the vault, a hundred years went by, up in the world. And he remembered what he heard when Ostap read to him out of the great book. And his soul grew bitter and sad at the sight of the world and its sorrow and evil, and he wished to tell people all that Ostap had read to him, so that here on earth also folk might live rightly and joyfully.

He went up to the folk he met on the road, and began telling them the happy truth of how folk live in the other world. And he said how on earth also people might live justly and with happiness.

But very few were ready to listen to him. They turned from him angrily, or told him to go off on his business, or took no notice of him at all, as if he had not been standing there and opening his mouth to tell them the good news. And of those who did listen to him, some did not believe him, others did not understand, and some even laughed at him.

He went with his good news from village to village through the world. And wandering, he came at last back to his own village. It was a rare cold night in autumn, and in his own village, he had no welcome, and stood in the road there by

his own house, without a bed, with no food, not knowing where to go next.

And Ivan went to his brother's grave, where the great oak grew that he had planted three hundred years before. He fell on his face on the ground, and said: "Let me come in to you, brother, for there is no place for me on earth. I can be of no use to anyone at all."

And the earth opened. And Ivan went down into the vault and greeted Ostap his brother. And the earth closed above them. And, while the earth goes on as badly as before, Ostap and Ivan sit in the vault, and read out of the great book by the light of wax candles. As one candle goes out, they light another, and read on, and with each candle the world is older by a hundred years—and no wiser.